When in Rome...

At home, Kelly had spent hours looking at Rome websites (or the cute Roman guys on them, anyway), and now, from the bus, she recognized the jagged ruins of the Colosseum, Rome's ancient stadium. She hoped it would be as impressive in real life as it looked online.

The bus turned through a set of iron gates with a brass sign posted on them: PROGRAMMA INTERNAZIONALE DI ROMA. The building wasn't enormous, but it was impressive: four stories high, in reddish stucco with lighter-colored details around the tall, arched windows framed with green shutters.

"It's even prettier than the pictures in the brochure," Kelly said. "Check out that terrace over there. That'll be the perfect place for sunbathing and soaking up the scenery."

"Or reading," Sheela said.

Kelly sighed. "You can't tell me we've just flown four thousand miles so you can stick your head in a book and ignore a view like this."

"Okay, okay. For once, I'm totally with you," Sheela answered. "This is absolutely beautiful."

Spontaneously, the girls reached out and squeezed each other's hands. They had arrived.

S.A.S.S.
STUDENTS ACROSS THE SEVEN SEAS

Getting the
Boot

Peggy Guthart Strauss

speak
An Imprint of Penguin Group (USA) Inc.

SPEAK
Published by the Penguin Group
Penguin Group (USA) Inc.,
345 Hudson Street, New York, New York 10014, U.S.A.
Penguin Group (Canada), 10 Alcorn Avenue, Toronto, Ontario, Canada M4V 3B2
(a division of Pearson Penguin Canada Inc.)
Penguin Books Ltd, 80 Strand, London WC2R 0RL, England
Penguin Ireland, 25 St Stephen's Green, Dublin 2, Ireland
(a division of Penguin Books Ltd)
Penguin Group (Australia), 250 Camberwell Road, Camberwell, Victoria 3124, Australia
(a division of Pearson Australia Group Pty Ltd)
Penguin Books India Pvt Ltd, 11 Community Centre, Panchsheel Park,
New Delhi - 110 017, India
Penguin Group (NZ), Cnr Airborne and Rosedale Roads, Albany, Auckland 1310,
New Zealand (a division of Pearson New Zealand Ltd)
Penguin Books (South Africa) (Pty) Ltd, 24 Sturdee Avenue, Rosebank, Johannesburg 2196,
South Africa

Registered Offices: Penguin Books Ltd, 80 Strand, London WC2R 0RL, England

Published by Speak, an imprint of Penguin Group (USA) Inc., 2005

3 5 7 9 10 8 6 4

Copyright © Peggy Guthart Strauss, 2005
All rights reserved
Interior art and design by Jeanine Henderson. Text set in Imago Book.

ISBN 978-0-14-240414-0

Printed in the United States of America

This book is dedicated, with many thanks, to Becky Guthart. Without her insightful comments and creative input, this book would have never been written.

Thanks, also, to Ivano Pulito, who generously provided me with tons of useful information about his real-life semester in Aventino.

And to my husband, Ed, for putting up with me.

Getting the Boot

Vatican City

Kelly's Rome

Trevi Fountain

Pantheon

Colosseum

Roman Forum

Bocca della Verità

Fiume Tevere

Trastevere

Aventino / PIR

Application

Students Across the Seven Seas Study Abroad Program

Name: Kelly Brandt

Age: 17

High School: Westlake High School

Hometown: Chicago, Illinois

Preferred Study Abroad Destination: Rome, Italy

1. Why are you interested in traveling abroad next year?

Answer: I am very interested in studying the ~~language of romance~~ Romance Languages and expect that visiting Italy will give me a greater appreciation for the diversity of our world.

(Truth: Are you kidding? Three words—men, leather, and fashion. Who WOULDN'T want to travel to a place that has the most fabulous of all three?)

2. How will studying abroad further develop your talents and interests?

Answer: I will apply what I've learned from Italian ~~couture~~ culture to my long-term career goal of becoming a fashion designer.

(Truth: My wardrobe will get an all-designer makeover.

I'll be a fashion goddess (hopefully one who's worshipped by legions of admiring Roman males!).)

3. Describe your extracurricular activities.

Answer: President of the Student Council, Dance Squad Captain, Drama Club President, Homecoming Court Three Years running, tennis, Pilates.

(Truth: Scoping out boys, plundering the discount racks for designer clothes, doing my friends' make-up, and begging my parents daily to let me go to Italy.)

4. Is there anything else you feel we should know about you?

Answer: I'm the kind of person who gets along with everybody. My outgoing personality will be a great asset to the S.A.S.S. program, and I look forward to sharing my enthusiasm for Italy with my fellow students. Also, I can guarantee that I'll be a student you will never forget!

(Truth: If you don't let me into this program, when I am a famous designer I will make sure that you NEVER get a discount on any of my very exclusive, very glamorous signature lines.)

Chapter One

Turbulence jolted Kelly Brandt out of a deep sleep as the captain announced their initial descent into Rome's Fiumicino Airport. Almost there! She looked at the view out the airplane window, expecting a fairy-tale scene below her. Instead, the neat squares of fields looked surprisingly like the Illinois farmland they had passed over on their takeoff from O'Hare.

Kelly could almost feel the Italian sunshine hitting her face. Rome was going to be awesome—delicious food, tons of culture, and shopping, shopping, shopping! She pictured handsome gondoliers rowing down moonlit canals

past chic Romans wearing cutting-edge European fashions. And there was absolutely no such thing as a bad slice of pizza. Who could live there and not end up worldly, sophisticated, and glamorous? She would return home in three months' time, a vision in flame-red lipstick and couture clothes, throwing around endearments like *cara* and *bella* without sounding like a pretentious ass.

Kelly yawned loudly and stretched her arms over her head, wondering just how long she had slept. Judging from the thick novel in her friend Sheela's lap—now halfway read—it had been quite a while. Kelly had sorely needed the rest.

The night before, her best friends, Starr and Tyffani, had thrown her a going-away party. Starr Santoro was legendary for throwing the best parties; she always attracted the hottest crowd, found the best DJs, and made kids from all over the area beg for invites. Going to a Starr party was like going to an exclusive club: If you didn't have the right look or know the right people, you couldn't get through the door. And the party she threw for Kelly's last night home had topped them all.

Normally, Sheela would never have made the invite list, and she wouldn't have cared a bit. But Kelly had insisted that Starr include her, and had begged Sheela to come along. Sheela would, after all, be Kelly's only tie to home once they got to Italy; it was key that the girls get along this summer.

Kelly had known Sheela Ramaswamy forever. Their dads had roomed together in college, and their families still got together every so often on weekends. Even though their crowds didn't mix much in school, the girls had a history that kept them together.

Sheela and Kelly had been inseparable in elementary school, but things changed in junior high. Kelly got braces, made it onto the dance team, and landed a plum role in the school play. All of a sudden she was surrounded by a tight new circle of friends, and had more and more excuses for spending less and less time with Sheela.

By the time they started high school, Sheela was every parent's dream—and every party girl's nightmare. She was responsible and mature, got fantastic grades, and stayed out of trouble. Instead of enjoying being sixteen and single with a spanking-new driver's license, Sheela was wasting the best years of her life on moldy books and the math team. If Kelly could convince her to loosen up and have some fun, maybe there was hope that they'd have a blast together in Italy.

When the two girls walked into the party, Starr and Tyff hugged Kelly as if it had been months, not hours, since they'd seen her.

"Our guest—*guests*—of honor have arrived!" Starr announced, ushering them in the door. "So Kel, are you ready for *bella* Roma?"

"The question is, is Roma ready for us?" Kelly laughed.

"Love your hair, Sheela," Tyff said, smiling at her.

Sheela's hand flew up to her head self-consciously. "Thanks. Kelly did it for me. And my makeup."

"Well, no wonder it looks fabulous," Starr said over her shoulder as she and Tyff ran off to greet some new arrivals.

"Since when do your buddies even know I exist, much less shower me with compliments?" Sheela whispered to Kelly.

"Since I told them that you have a pierced nipple and your boyfriend's name tattooed on your butt, and that that's why you're so shy about taking your clothes off in gym."

Sheela burst out laughing at the utter ridiculousness of this scenario. "He must be quite a guy if I'm branding his name onto my ass. Is he cute at least?"

"Beautiful. He's a Portuguese bad boy with long black hair." She gave Sheela's dark locks a flip. "And a Harley. Too bad you're gonna ditch him for a Roman hottie on a Vespa."

The way Kelly said it, it had almost seemed possible.

They made their way to the bar, where Kelly, ignoring Sheela's anxious expression, poured them each a glass of punch. Kelly's father was a corporate attorney, and he had developed a technique for making sure his daughter behaved herself at parties. Before going out, she had to sign a contract banning drugs and drinking. It was an effective approach, mostly, but Kelly had become expert at tweaking the rules here and there.

"This is spiked," Sheela said. "Didn't you promise your parents you wouldn't drink tonight?"

"Relax," Kelly answered. "I have a system. Take a few sips, then hold the glass all night. That way, nobody bugs you." Kelly waved at someone on the other side of the room. "Come on. There's someone I want you to meet."

"Freddy, Sheela. Sheela, Freddy." Kelly put a death grip on Sheela's arm so she wouldn't run away and whispered in her ear. "One gorgeous Portuguese biker boy, with my compliments." She smiled into her friend's scarlet face.

Kelly watched as Sheela cast a furtive glance at Freddy. He smiled and reached out to shake her hand. "According to Kelly, we've been dating for years. Why don't you tell me about yourself?"

Kelly let the two of them talk while she perched on the arm of a nearby couch and flirted with a few football players from school. One of them held up a lit joint. "Kel, you want a hit?"

Kelly wrinkled her nose. "Nope, not my thing. Actually, all the smoke in here is making my allergies go crazy. What I *need* to do is dance." She grabbed a partner off the couch and waved to Sheela. "Have fun, you crazy kids." She spun on her stilettos and took off.

Kelly sighed happily at the memory. The party had been

a total success. Even though Sheela had left early to finish packing, it was obvious that she had enjoyed herself. Kelly hadn't seen her laugh so much since they were little. And she'd never seen her dance before, much less with a guy. Kelly's biggest gamble, enlisting Freddy, a pal from work, to play Sheela's boyfriend, had worked like a charm.

It was an absolutely perfect send-off until the very end of the evening, when Tyff had burst into tears.

"Summer won't be the same without you. Who will I go to the beach with? The parties are totally gonna suck." She snuffled pathetically. "I'll miss you."

"Yeah, and who will *I* go shopping with?" Starr demanded. "I mean, Tyff's okay with shoes, but she can't accessorize to save her life."

Kelly put her arm around Tyff. "C'mon, guys. It's only three months. You'll be back in bags and belts in no time."

"It's not just three months," Tyffani whined. "You'll come back totally changed, and you won't want to have anything to do with us senior year. And then we'll go off to college and this will all be over."

A wave of nostalgia washed over Kelly as she gazed out the plane window; she wished all of her friends could have come to Italy with her. She had no regrets about saying good-bye to life in the dull suburbs, but she would sorely miss her crew. Exploring Rome had to be a thousand times more fun than hanging out in Chicago, but doing it alone was no good. She was thankful Sheela would be there with her, even if the girl's social skills needed a major boost.

Sheela had reverted to her bookworm ways the instant she'd left Starr's house. In fact, if she hadn't been turning a page every now and then, Kelly would have checked her pulse. It was a shame, because Sheela could be lots of fun, on the rare occasions she let her guard down. She had a dry kind of wit that cracked Kelly up and a simple, direct style that was a nice break from some of the posers at school. Kelly hoped that at some point this summer, she could convince her old friend to enjoy herself a little.

Kelly actually considered it her duty to kick up their friendship a notch. After all, if it hadn't been for Sheela, Kelly would never have found out about the S.A.S.S. program, or the Programma Internazionale di Roma. S.A.S.S. was a study-abroad program for American girls that placed them in schools all around the world, and the Programma was Sheela's school of choice. Its director, Dr. Timothy Wainwright, had been Mr. Ramaswamy's adviser in grad school. Dr. Wainwright had sent Mr. R a copy of the brochure with Sheela in mind, but the moment Kelly had spied Sheela reading it in the high-school cafeteria, she had been intrigued. Even now, months later, she still couldn't stop looking through the brochure. Kelly pulled it out of her carry-on bag and flipped through it for the umpteenth time.

The cover featured a panoramic view of some ancient ruins with the sun setting majestically behind them.

Smaller photo insets showed happy-looking teenagers strolling down quaint, cobblestone streets, eating gelato, hiking in the countryside, and engaged in animated discussion in a classroom. Inside, a headline announced, EARN SCHOOL CREDITS WHILE IMMERSING YOURSELF IN THE HISTORY, LANGUAGE, AND CULTURE OF ITALY.

"You know, in a couple of hours we'll actually be there," Sheela said. "I think you can ditch the brochure already."

"I can't help it," Kelly said. "I'm just so freaking excited. What do you think the dorms are gonna be like? I'm picturing something straight out of MTV *Cribs*!"

Sheela snorted. "Except they don't have homework on *Cribs*. Seriously, Kelly, it's a school, not a spa. You're actually going to have to do some work, you know."

Kelly groaned. "Don't remind me. My parents certainly haven't let me forget." She flashed her most brilliant smile. "Luckily, I have a genius at my disposal."

"Are you saying the Ramaswamy SAT prep course wasn't enough for you?" Sheela picked up her book again. "High-quality wisdom like mine is going to cost you from now on."

Kelly laughed. "I'll keep that in mind." More seriously, she added, "I already totally owe you, Sheela."

It hadn't been easy convincing her parents—or the S.A.S.S. coordinator, or Dr. Wainwright, for that matter—that she could cut it in such a rigorous academic program, but Kelly had waged a long, hard campaign. Initially, she was wait-listed as a S.A.S.S. candidate. But then she'd been inspired to try a backdoor approach and had asked Sheela's dad for Dr. Wainwright's e-mail address. And it had worked. She brought her grades up, cut way back on socializing, and, with Sheela's help, got a far better score on her SATs than anyone would have expected. And she made sure that Dr. W was aware of each of her accomplishments. She had earned her acceptance fair and square, and now she was going to enjoy every minute of her summer abroad.

Sheela smiled slyly. "You can buy me a *stracciatella* gelato for paybacks."

Kelly blinked. "What the hell is that?"

"It's vanilla gelato with chocolate chips."

"You got it."

The plane took another gentle dip downward. Kelly pulled her purse up onto her lap and felt around inside. Mirror, brush, lip gloss, blush, mascara.

Sheela looked at her quizzically. "What are you getting all dolled up for? It's six o'clock in the morning in Rome."

Kelly smiled and shrugged. "I want to make a good impression on Italy, that's all."

"On Italian men, more like."

"Yeah, well, in celebrity mags, paparazzi are always snapping shots of stars as they get off planes. It's important to always look your best—you never know who you might bump into." She reached over to smooth Sheela's seat back–induced hair frizz and got her hand smacked.

"If Orlando Bloom happens to be loitering around the airport at the crack of dawn, I'll be out of luck. Otherwise, lay off."

Kelly looked out the window as the plane descended for landing. The weather was thick and overcast, and the plane had to circle before finally bumping onto the runway. As soon as the seat-belt sign went off, Kelly jumped up so fast she nearly blasted a hole in the overhead compartment. The girls hoisted their carry-on bags and followed the crowd to the baggage carousels.

Sheela consulted a stack of well-thumbed papers. "I guess most of the other kids are coming in on early-morning flights, too. They're sending two buses, one at eight, one at nine-thirty." She checked her watch: 6:45 A.M., Rome time. "Looks like we're in the right terminal to meet the first bus."

Kelly was barely listening. Instead, she was scanning the crowd gathered around the luggage carousels. It was easy enough to spot the Americans, but she couldn't figure out whether the others were real Italians or not. Many wore jeans and T-shirts. A group of seedy-looking taxi drivers circled around, waving signs and pinching cigarettes between tobacco-stained fingers as they searched for fares.

It took the girls quite a while to collect their suitcases and go through customs. Kelly was at a total loss when it came to understanding the customs officials, and Sheela had to do all the talking. After what seemed like forever, they collapsed onto a bench outside to wait for the bus.

"Now I know why they call this flight the red-eye," Kelly said, yawning.

"I know. I feel like we've been traveling for days." Sheela glanced at Kelly. "Hey, where's the locket your mom gave you?"

Kelly gasped, her hand flying up to her neck. She pulled the chain out from underneath her shirt. "Oh, thank God." She elbowed Sheela. "You scared the crap out of me. My parents would kill me if I lost this."

"Sorry. Can I see it again?"

Kelly proudly held out the locket. Her parents had given it to her as a going-away present when they dropped her off at the airport. It was an antique that had belonged to her mom's mother. Kelly carefully opened the shiny gold lid, running her fingers over the swirling script initials etched on its surface. The inside held an old black-and-white photo of her grandmother and a new shot of her parents.

"Wow, your grandmother looked just like you when she was young," Sheela said.

"Yeah, and my mother says I'm as full of piss and vine-gar as she was," Kelly said, laughing. "I still can't believe Mom gave this to me. She's worn it ever since Grandma died last year. But my granddad bought it for my grand-mother when they were on their honeymoon in Rome, so I guess my mother thought it was a sign or something. She

says it will be like my grandmother is watching over me when I wear it. When she was alive, Grandma never took it off. And neither will I."

Sheela glanced down at her watch and stood up. "It's almost eight. The bus should be here soon."

Kelly carefully tucked the locket back under her shirt, grabbed her suitcases, and followed Sheela outside. The sun was burning off the last bits of fog, and the air was getting downright steamy. A man approached them, waving his arms toward the parking area and shouting something Kelly couldn't understand.

Sheela answered him politely, "No, *grazie*."

"Is that our bus driver?" Kelly asked.

"Nope. A bootleg cabbie."

"If this bus doesn't come soon, that might be an option," Kelly muttered.

Just then a little blue bus with a sign in the window reading PROGRAMMA INTERNAZIONALE DI ROMA zipped by, and slowed to a stop a short distance past them. Kelly and Sheela jumped up and rushed down the sidewalk as fast as their bags would allow. A small cluster of similarly burdened teens was already lining up to board.

There was a punk/Goth girl with spiky jet-black hair and thick, smudgy eyeliner, an outdoorsy-looking guy with a huge hiker's frame pack strapped to his back, and two girls whom Starr would have described as "granolas." As they got closer, Sheela's face froze into a petrified grin.

"God, I hate being sociable," she muttered.

Kelly reached out and squeezed Sheela's arm. "Relax. They're just people. Nobody's going to bite your head off." She smiled. "With your brains and my personality, we can't go wrong. Promise me you'll try to enjoy yourself."

Sheela gave her a grateful nod and took a few deep breaths. "Okay, let's do it."

Chapter Two

Located in the lush residential neighborhood of Aventino, the school facilities offer modern conveniences such as air-conditioning, Internet access, and a student lounge with television and refrigerator. Within short walking distance, you will find cafés, pizzerias, bakeries, and a supermarket. The neighborhood is served by Metro Linea B (Circo Massimo stop), as well as several bus lines.

Kelly put the school brochure down and glanced out the window as the bus entered a big highway congested with morning-rush traffic. Little cars zipped around them on every side. The dozen kids filling the little van were surprisingly quiet, battling to stay awake after their long flights. She opened her window so she could take in every detail of the scenery.

Soon they pulled off the *autostrada* and were driving through Rome itself. Kelly had never seen so many buildings that looked so old. There were no tall skyscrapers or modern office buildings, just little brick or stucco structures that mostly seemed to be apartment buildings or stores. It was so quaint, just like the pictures in the brochure!

Many shopkeepers were raising the gates of their businesses, sweeping the sidewalks, and opening their awnings. They passed a deli window filled with hanging salamis and huge wheels of cheese, then a greengrocer's, with baskets of bright fruits and vegetables lined up out front. Strings of dried herbs hung between them like necklaces. The air was filled with the scent of brewing coffee and baking bread, making Kelly realize how hungry she was.

The bus wove through a hilly, quiet neighborhood. Kelly noticed that the apartment buildings had given way to nice houses with landscaped gardens and walls surrounding them. Sheela pointed out the window. "You can see a lot of the city from here. That's St. Peter's, where the Vatican is, and that's the Tiber River running through the city."

Kelly looked out on the panorama that stretched in front of them, dominated by the river and the ornate dome of

the Vatican beyond it. "So is the Tiber where the gondolas are?" Kelly's dreamy vision of riding in one of the romantic-looking boats was still fresh in her mind.

Sheela shook her head. "Gondolas are up north in Venice."

"Are you sure? They don't have them anywhere else?"

"I'm positive. It's just a Venice thing. The Venetians use them to navigate the canals. The whole city is built on water, not like Rome at all."

Kelly shook her head. "Fine, but if you tell me that gondoliers aren't handsome and don't serenade their passengers, I'm gonna be pissed."

"As far as I know, they're all gorgeous and have voices like angels," Sheela replied, smiling.

"Well, what about the leaning tower of Pisa? Can we see that from here?"

"Not unless you have superhuman vision. Pisa is a city in Tuscany, also north of here."

"Of Pisa. I get it," Kelly muttered sheepishly.

They passed a beautiful little park where people were soaking in the view of the city from benches or strolling among what looked to Kelly like orange trees.

"That must be Parco Savello," Sheela told her. "I read about it in a guidebook. There was once a castle here owned by a really wealthy family. The gates lead out to a church called Santa Sabina that's supposed to be beautiful. When we get some free time we *have* to go check that out."

Kelly had thought that their PIR dorm would be in the heart of vibrant Rome, with shops, restaurants, and tons of people right outside her door. All of the websites she'd looked at had shown the bustling city center. It was pretty up here, but it seemed almost as sleepy as the suburbs. At least the houses looked swanky; there was a Mercedes parked in almost every driveway they passed.

Next to her, Sheela seemed to be getting more excited by the minute. "There's the Circus Maximus, where they held chariot races in ancient Roman times. We're going to be close enough to walk down there whenever we want! This totally beats selling steel-belted girdles at the mall." Sheela had worked at a lingerie store the summer before, measuring old ladies for bras. She still hadn't recovered from the trauma.

Kelly shrugged. "It just looks like a bunch of grass to me."

"How do you think you'd look if you were two thousand years old?" Sheela retorted.

Kelly smiled. This was the feisty Sheela she loved spending time with. Maybe there was hope for the girl yet.

At home, Kelly had spent hours looking at Rome websites (or the cute Roman guys on them, anyway), and now she recognized the jagged ruins of the Colosseum, Rome's ancient stadium. She hoped it would be as impressive in real life as it looked online.

The bus turned through a set of iron gates with a brass

sign posted on them: PROGRAMMA INTERNAZIONALE DI ROMA. The building wasn't enormous, but it was impressive: four stories high, in reddish stucco with lighter-colored details around the tall, arched windows framed with green shutters.

"It's even prettier than the pictures in the brochure," Kelly said. "Check out that terrace over there. That'll be the perfect place for sunbathing and soaking up the scenery."

"Or reading," Sheela said.

Kelly sighed. "You can't tell me we've just flown four thousand miles so you can stick your head in a book and ignore a view like this."

"Okay, okay. For once, I'm totally with you," Sheela answered. "This is absolutely beautiful."

Spontaneously, the girls reached out and squeezed each other's hands. They had arrived.

Dr. Wainwright was waiting to greet the group as they entered the cool, dark building. He looked exactly like a professor type: tall and somewhat stooped, probably from too many years of leaning over books, with a long face and thinning, sandy-colored hair. Only his outfit, Bermuda shorts, sandals, and a golf shirt, didn't fit Kelly's image. His light blue eyes sparkled with excitement as the group straggled in with their bags.

"Welcome! Leave your belongings here. The custodial

staff will bring your luggage upstairs for you. Just make
sure they're properly labeled." He passed around a stack of
labels and markers, gazing at each student intently as he
greeted them.

He made a beeline for Sheela, exclaiming, "Yes, I see the
resemblance. How is your dear dad?" And when he got to
Kelly, he grinned broadly. "Miss Brandt, it's a true pleasure
to meet you. Your e-mails kept me in stitches all winter! All
seventy of them."

"My pleasure, too, sir." Kelly shot him her best pep-rally
smile.

"If you show as much persistence in your studies as you
did convincing me to accept you into the program, you'll
wow us all." He chuckled.

"Seventy?" Sheela whispered to Kelly, looking mortified.
"You sent Dr. Wainwright seventy e-mails?"

"He's exaggerating," Kelly answered. "It was closer to
fifty. When S.A.S.S. wait-listed me, I had to go straight to
the top. My dad always says that juries have short memories. If you don't keep reminding them, they forget your
argument. It's the same principle."

"And Miss Ramaswamy," Dr. Wainwright continued,
beaming at Sheela. "I'm thrilled to have you in the program. Your dad is still one of the best students I've ever
had the privilege to work with. Welcome."

"Thank you," Sheela said, shooting Kelly another scold-

ing look. Kelly couldn't have cared less. All those e-mails had bought her a ticket to Rome, and Dr. Wainwright obviously thought they were funny.

Dr. Wainwright addressed everyone. "Tonight, we'll take our first journey together, to a genuine Roman *osteria*. We'll share a good meal and get to know each other. I hope you will soon start to feel as at home here as I do." His eyes crinkled when he smiled. "We're still waiting for a dozen of your compatriots to arrive, so I think the first thing everyone should do is grab a bite to eat downstairs. Signora Peretti, our wonderful cook, has prepared a restorative breakfast for you. Once everyone has arrived and had a chance to settle in, we'll have a brief orientation to introduce you to the staff and facilities. Then you'll have some free time for a much-needed rest."

Fourteen kids traipsed down a narrow wooden staircase to the dining room. Kelly hadn't been sure what Italians ate for breakfast, but it looked pretty normal: yogurt, a couple of healthy-looking cereals, juice, and a big basket of rolls. Best of all, the cook had put out an urn of coffee and a pitcher of steamed milk. Cappuccino for breakfast! How bad could this place be?

After they ate, the janitor, Signor Peretti, who spoke almost no English, led them upstairs to show them their dorm rooms. Now that her stomach was full, Kelly was yearning for a nap and a shower. They climbed the steps back to the main floor, and then continued up a wider set of stone stairs. "Floor one—class-a-room," the old man said, waving his arm down the hallway. They kept climbing. "Floor two—more class-a-room, computers *e* lounge." Another floor. Sweat dripped down Kelly's back. Didn't they have an elevator in this place? "Floor three—boy rooms." The guys dispersed down the hall, looking at cards posted on each door for their names. The little man skittered up the final flight effortlessly. "Floor four—girl rooms." He nodded, and was gone.

"So unfair! Why do we have to climb all the way up to the top of the building?" Kelly muttered. Goth Girl also seemed pissed, and muttered something about an "archaic, paternalistic culture" that Kelly didn't fully catch.

Sheela puffed up behind her. "The queen of Pilates and dance squad is complaining about four measly flights of stairs? I thought you could walk that in your sleep."

"I'm so tired I feel like I'm sleepwalking," Kelly said, searching for her luggage in the hallway. She hoisted her two huge suitcases, stooping under their weight.

"Exactly how many pairs of shoes did you bring, anyway?" Sheela asked, amused by Kelly's struggle.

"As many as I need, so cease and desist with the wisecracks."

Sheela laughed. "Uh-oh, you're using your dad's lawyer lingo now. You must be crabby."

Kelly opted to ignore Sheela's teasing and set off to find her new digs. The room was at the end of the hall, next to

an emergency stairwell and a bathroom, both good things to have nearby. And she and Sheela were roommates, as she had requested.

There were two small bedrooms, and Kelly immediately started scoping them out to see which had the better view. Sheela followed her in, talking to another girl. She smiled at Kelly and said, "This is Lisa, one of our suite mates."

Kelly plopped down on the sofa. Suite? They had to be kidding. As it was, each room was about the size of a girls' bathroom stall at Westlake High. "Hi, Lisa," she managed, curling her lips into a forced smile. Lisa had a head full of dark, frizzy hair and wore a drab tank top made of some overly natural fiber. Kelly would have to help her out with that hair; she wondered if she could find a flat iron in Rome. She looked at Lisa again and saw more black hair hanging out of her armpits. Gross.

Lisa made a beeline for the room Kelly had earmarked and threw her bag, a fake tapestry number with ANIMALS ARE OUR FRIENDS, NOT OUR FOOD and SAVE THE RAIN FORESTS decals stuck all over it, onto one of the beds. "Are you sharing with me?" She smiled eagerly at Sheela.

"Um, I kind of already promised Kelly that we'd share," Sheela replied.

Lisa shrugged and began pulling things out of her suitcase. Kelly couldn't resist watching—half the contents seemed to be packages of food and jars of vitamins. She picked one up. "Amino acids? I remember those from biology. Why do you have them?"

Lisa gave her a benevolent smile. "I'm vegan, so I have to make sure I have proper nutritional support while I'm here. You'd be surprised how many things that seem like they're fine have milk or eggs in them."

"You came all the way to Italy and you're not going to eat any cheese or gelato? I mean, half the reason I'm here is for the pizza."

Lisa frowned. "Taking milk from cows without their permission is a violation of their rights."

Kelly laughed. "Next time, I'll be sure to ask."

Lisa was not amused. "Do you understand that when you eat meat and wear leather, you are responsible for the murder of animals? Have you ever had a pet? You didn't eat him, did you? It's the same exact thing."

Kelly sensed she wasn't going to win this argument, so she made a quick excuse and bailed. In their room, Sheela was already laying neat little stacks of underwear and shirts on her bed. "So we can work this two ways," Sheela said. "Either we each take two dresser drawers and share the closet space, or I can use one and you can use the other."

"Only one dresser and one closet? Are you sure?" But there they were, clear as day; unless there was some secret hole in the floor, the room was way too tiny to be

hiding any extra storage space. And, naturally, they were the puniest closet and dresser imaginable. Kelly looked at her two enormous suitcases with a sinking feeling.

"Let's share both, I guess," she finally said. Sheela nodded amenably and kept on organizing, putting her toiletries into a little basket. Kelly pulled the latest issue of *Glamour* from her bag along with her sketchbook and flopped down on her bed. She loved scouting out the hottest runway looks and drawing her own designs.

"Aren't you going to start unpacking?" Sheela asked. "We won't have much time once classes start."

Kelly made a face. "Are you kidding? I'm way too wiped to do anything but veg right now. I'll unpack tonight."

The final member of their rooming group timidly stuck her head in the doorway. "Hello? Are you guys Sheela and Kelly?"

She was tiny, with wire-rim glasses and long, blond hair pulled back in a limp ponytail. "I'm Minnie."

Minnie certainly was mini, but Kelly decided to keep that joke to herself. "Have you met Lisa yet? You two will be roommates."

Minnie smiled enthusiastically. "Oh, yes. We sat together on the bus. She's great." She looked around their little cell. "We're gonna have the neatest time together, you guys! I'll see you later."

"The *neatest*, absolutely," Kelly murmured under her breath.

She could feel Sheela's disapproving eyes on her. "Just because they're not fashion plates doesn't make them bad people," she said. "Try to keep an open mind for once, will you?"

"I'll do my best," Kelly answered lightly. Time to change the subject, quick. "Where do you suppose the AC is in here? I'm about to die from heat prostration." She climbed onto her bed and put her hand over the little vented box attached to the ceiling. The faintest breeze was coming out of it. "Please tell me this isn't it."

Sheela got up and waved her hand in front of the vent. "Could be. These old buildings weren't made for central air, and I've read that Europeans don't much like it, anyway."

Kelly groaned. No air-conditioning, no elevator, no storage space. This place was a total scam. She jumped up and began rummaging through her backpack.

"What are you looking for?"

"This." Kelly held up her Italian dictionary. "As soon as we can get out of here, we're buying the biggest, strongest *ventilatore* in Rome!"

After taking a few hours to unpack and rest, all twenty-six students assembled in the second-floor lounge for orientation. Kelly noted the big-screen TV and DVD player with satisfaction. And there were two big, comfy couches to stretch out on. She'd be spending a lot of time on those.

Dr. Wainwright walked in with three other adults, presumably teachers, and began his welcome spiel. Kelly wanted to pay attention, but she found herself scanning each member of the group instead. *Teeny roommate with tree-hugger roommate. Outdoorsy guy from the bus. Goth Girl—could be interesting, or really weird. Lots of kids Starr would describe as "bookish." Hello—megacute blond guy.* Kelly made eye contact and smiled, and Cute Boy returned the gesture. Great smile and gorgeous teeth, too.

Dr. Wainwright was droning on, sounding suspiciously like her parents. "Violence doesn't happen here much, but you want to keep your wits about you, and be very careful with your wallets and purses. There are a lot of pickpockets and purse snatchers in this city, so you're best off carrying only copies of important papers. If you can get along without carrying a bag, that's ideal. Otherwise, wear it with the strap diagonally across your chest."

Easy enough. Kelly glanced over at Cute Boy again. Was that a tattoo peeking out of his sleeve? She couldn't wait to ask him about it. And maybe give one of his biceps a squeeze for good measure.

"Ladies, it's also best if you explore the city in small groups rather than on your own, especially after dark. Unfortunately, some Roman men can be very forward with women, tourists in particular. I have no personal experience, of course," Dr. Wainwright added, his eyes crinkling.

"But I'm told the best way to cope is to make no eye contact and walk purposefully."

He continued with a bunch of everyday stuff—Internet use, laundry, cell-phone rentals—plus house rules and curfew time, which was eleven o'clock weeknights (or twenty-three hours, as they put it in Europe) and 1 A.M. weekends. Not too bad.

Then it was time to meet the resident staff members. While many of the program instructors lived off campus, a few, along with Dr. Wainwright and Signor and Signora Peretti, the janitor and the cook, lived in a smaller building just behind the school. Kelly wondered whether their rooms had air-conditioning.

"This is my A-team," Dr. Wainwright said. "They will accompany you on field trips both inside and outside Rome, and will be available, along with me, to provide you with any advice and assistance you need."

Each person stepped forward modestly as Dr. Wainwright introduced them.

The first was Steve, a jovial, red-haired guy from Wisconsin who looked like a grown-up frat boy. He would be teaching classes in ancient history and archaeology. Out of the corner of her eye, Kelly could see Sheela nodding approvingly; archaeology was totally her thing.

Next up was Marco, the language instructor. He spoke English with a charming British-Italian accent, and he had

really nice, shiny black hair. Too bad he was a teacher—a cute, smart Italian guy was exactly what Kelly was looking for. Maybe she'd hold off on the blond dude for a little while; it would be so much cooler to date a European.

The third person caught Kelly's attention immediately. This was the sort of chic, striking Italian woman Kelly wanted to emulate. She had large gray eyes, reddish-brown curls that tumbled just to her shoulders, and a warm smile. But her perfect posture and regal bearing also gave her the air of someone you didn't want to mess with. When she introduced herself as Andrea (pronounced the Italian way, *on-DRAY-uh*), Kelly was surprised to hear a plain old American accent. Andrea was finishing her Ph.D. in art history, and was teaching classes not only in that, but also in studio arts. *Now you're talking,* Kelly thought. *Sitting in a shady park, painting the pretty scenery, or sketching in some nice, cool air-conditioned gallery.*

Dr. Wainwright stepped forward again. "We have many other teachers who live off campus, and guest instructors will come in frequently to give lectures and workshops on subjects ranging from cooking to architecture to Mussolini. Also, summer classes are open to students who attend this school during the year, so there will be around twenty other pupils in class every day. That will give you a nice opportunity to meet kids from all over the globe." Hanging out with the jet set! Exactly what Kelly had in mind.

"That's it—intros over," Dr. Wainwright finished. "Let's go get some of the best Italian food you've ever tasted!"

The entire group walked over to a restaurant in the neighborhood, where Dr. Wainwright had reserved a back room. Kelly quickly noticed a couple of empty spaces near Cute Boy. But first, she headed over to Sheela, who was waving at Kelly to join her and their suite mates.

"Thanks for saving me a spot," Kelly said, "but there's someone at the other end of the table who requires my attention."

Sheela shrugged. "I guess he's cute, if you like that type. But I thought you had your heart set on a native."

"Just keeping my options open." Kelly smiled and swung her hair over her shoulder. "*Buon appetito.*"

Kelly strode confidently toward Cute Boy, noting that his broad shoulders looked just as good from the back as they did from the front. "Mind if I sit here?"

C.B. shooed the guy next to him down a seat and patted the chair. "It's all yours. I'm Joe, and my roommate here is Rodney." Rodney, an almost-as-hunky African-American guy, nodded absently, already deep into his first plate of pasta.

Kelly gestured toward the buffet table. "Back in Chicago, my favorite Italian food is deep-dish pizza. I don't know what half this stuff is."

Joe flashed a smile. "I don't even care what it is, as long

as it's pasta. Where I come from, carbo-loading is practically against the law."

"And where is that?" Kelly asked.

"Southern Cal," Joe replied. "Malibu. The surfing is great, but there's only so much sashimi and tofu one person can eat."

Kelly wrinkled her nose. "I hate that kind of stuff."

"Yeah, and staying off it obviously hasn't done you any harm." Joe grinned flirtatiously. "Ready to hit the buffet and break a few laws with me?"

"Bring it on," Kelly answered, beaming back into his tan face.

Kelly filled her plate, inhaling the aroma of fresh basil and garlic. Cute boys, great food, and three months abroad. It couldn't get any better than this.

Chapter Three

To: kelcat@email.com
From: starrgirl@email.com
Subject: Missing you

Hi Kel,

Just in case you're wondering, the summer is going to be a total disaster. Tyffani and I went to the mall yesterday, but we could hardly bring ourselves to buy anything without you. Tyff has been moping NONSTOP. You better e-mail us with the scoop on Rome. It's your duty as my

best friend to tell me everything about the Italian boys you meet over there!

Starr

The first day of orientation, Marco took everybody on a tour of the Forum. Kelly and Sheela walked over the rutted cobblestones, looking at the ancient ruins in amazement. "This was the heart of ancient Roman society," Marco told them. "In the Forum, Romans celebrated, worshiped, orated, and governed."

"This is amazing," Sheela whispered to Kelly as they walked past the court buildings and temples. "So much history happened here. I'll bet that's where Caesar's senators murdered him." She pointed to a spot where several bouquets of flowers had been laid.

Kelly winced. "I'll tell you what's murder; walking around on these cobblestones."

"And whose fault is that? Leave it to you to wear kitten heels to the Forum."

Despite her achy feet, Kelly laughed. "I'm proud of you! You correctly used an actual fashion term!"

Sheela nodded modestly. "We nerds call it osmosis. After hanging around with you all these years, it was inevitable that something would sink in. Tell my friends at home and I'll kill you."

"Hey, babe," a voice behind Kelly said. An arm wrapped around her waist, and Kelly turned to find Joe.

"Shh." Kelly put a finger to her lips jokingly. "We're supposed to be learning about the Forum."

"Yeah, right," said Joe, playing along. He leaned forward with a mock-serious expression, pretending to hang on Marco's every word.

"The Romans also shopped, ate, drank, hung out with their friends, and went to the health spa here," Marco said. "This was probably the first mall in the world."

"Where's the food court?" Joe called out, giving Kelly a companionable elbow in the ribs. She cracked up, noticing from the corner of her eye that Sheela's expression had turned to stone.

Marco seemed equally unamused, so Joe continued his satirical running commentary in a whisper. But even at that level, Kelly could tell that Sheela was getting exasperated.

"I'm going to catch up with Minnie," Sheela whispered abruptly. She worked her way to the other side of the group before Kelly could answer.

"What's with her?" Joe asked, watching her take off.

"Sheela's really into history, that's all. She takes this pretty seriously."

"Good thing we don't have that problem, huh?"

Kelly smiled mischievously. "Yes, a very good thing." This place was interesting, but after a while Marco's stories all

started to sound the same. And the broiling sun wasn't helping Kelly concentrate any more than Joe's wisecracks.

After what seemed like hours, the group left the Forum and made the short walk to the Colosseum.

"This was the giant sports arena of ancient Rome," Marco told them. "Those days, entertainment revolved around killing and mutilation. Gladiators fought gladiators, criminals were forced to fight each other to the death, and wild animals often got thrown into the mix, for a little extra fun."

"What a bunch of sickos," Kelly whispered to Joe, who obviously loved every gory detail. "Lisa must be having a stroke about the animal thing."

Joe shrugged. "She's the one with hairy pits, right? Man, did you end up with a bunch of loser roommates. Maybe she'll be so offended that she'll have to go home. That would be a shame."

After lunch, Andrea took over for Marco and led the group for a walk along the Aurelian Wall, which surrounded and protected ancient Rome from invaders. Kelly's ears perked up as soon as Andrea started talking. Andrea was dressed in a chic linen pantsuit that was perfect for the hot day.

"Great," Joe muttered in Kelly's ear. "More useless information. I would so much rather be catching some z's right now."

"Shush," Kelly ordered. "I want to hear what she's saying."

Kelly moved toward the front of the group as Andrea stopped in front of a small stone building.

"This temple is dedicated to a great figure from mythology. See if you can guess who he is. His father was a god, his mother a mortal. In a fit of madness, he killed his own wife and children and was given twelve labors to atone for his deed. Anybody?"

Kelly's hand shot up. She couldn't wait to show Andrea that she'd studied up for this trip.

Andrea nodded at her. "Yes, Kelly?"

"It's obvious," Kelly said. "The guy with the weird heel. The word *kill* is in his name. Achilles."

Kelly heard muffled giggles throughout the group, and her face flamed.

"Good guess, Kelly," Andrea said. "Anyone else?"

Lisa's hand shot up. "Hercules, son of Zeus," she said smugly.

"That's correct," Andrea said. She went on to explain the temple's history, but Kelly was too embarrassed to pay attention. It was only when the group stepped inside a second little building that Kelly realized she recognized it. "*Roman Holiday!*" she burst out. Everybody looked at her like she was nuts, except for Andrea, who smiled.

"You're absolutely right. Has anyone else seen the movie?" A couple of kids raised their hands sheepishly. Kelly silently thanked her parents for renting it the night she

finally got her acceptance letter from the S.A.S.S. program.

"Why don't you tell everyone what it was about?"

Kelly used her practiced, drama-club voice. "It's about this teen princess visiting Rome who gets sick of being royalty and runs away. Since she's really chic and beautiful, naturally she attracts the attention of a hot young reporter, who takes her all over the city. Then, of course, they fall in love."

Kelly finished, looked up at Joe through her thick eyelashes, and smiled. For the first time all day, she felt smart.

"This is the Bocca della Veritá, or the Mouth of Truth." Andrea pointed to the fierce stone face mounted on the wall. "It's most likely a two-thousand-year-old manhole cover, but medieval legend had it that if a liar stuck his or her hand into the mouth, it would get snapped off by this guy's jaws." She stuck her hand in the mouth and yelled in alarm. A couple of kids jumped. "That's what freaked out Audrey Hepburn in *Roman Holiday*, and it probably still freaks out at least one person every single day." She removed her untouched hand and laughed.

As the group filed out of the portico, Joe grabbed Kelly's arm to hold her back. He placed her hand inside the Mouth of Truth.

"So, Kelly"—Joe leaned toward her—"do you have a boyfriend?"

Kelly laughed. That was another question she knew she could answer.

"Not yet," she said, and they both smiled.

To: starrgirl@email.com
From: kelcat@email.com
Subject: Rome-ance

Dear Starr,

Wassup? I am so tired it's ridiculous. The past few days, all we've done is walk, walk, walk. Our neighborhood is up on this hill, and it looks like we'll be covering every inch of it.

It's really pretty here in Aventino. Last night the director, Dr. Wainwright (who's very cool), took us to this public rose garden near our school for a concert. We got a private tour of the place first, which was okay, and then had to listen to boring classical music for an hour. Sheela loved it, duh.

Luckily, Rome has a super-romantic atmosphere, because I met the most amazing guy!!! His name is Joe, and he's gorgeous. Best of all, he's a for-real surfer, from Southern California!!! We've been really busy with orientation, but I've gotten to hang out with him a bit. Hoping to hang out a lot more . . .

Tell me EVERYTHING going on there. I miss you guys sooo much!!! Gotta go. Talk to you in a few days.

Ciao,

Kel

To: kelcat@email.com
From: starrgirl@email.com
Subject: RE: Rome-ance

Kel,

You go all the way to Rome and fall for a guy from California? I guess that means more cute Roman boys for me when it's my turn to go! I can live with that. Now let's talk about something really important...how's the shopping?

Starr

Classes were starting the next day, and Kelly had convinced Sheela to go shopping with her for school supplies. In the first hour, Kelly bought an adorable pair of strappy sandals (no heels this time!) and a baby tee from a street vendor that said CIAO on it. When Sheela finally pointed out to her that neither strictly qualified as a "school supply," Kelly relented and agreed to go into a stationery store.

The first thing Kelly grabbed was a handful of brightly colored pens. "Aren't they perfect? I'm getting a different color for each class. That way all my notes will be organized."

"Speaking as your oldest friend and roommate," Sheela said, "it's going to take a lot more than colored pens to keep you organized."

"Well, whatever. Maybe the bright colors will keep me from nodding off in history."

Kelly scanned her class schedule to see what else she needed. She had assured her parents she would work hard this summer, and it was important that her course load look serious. But she was hoping looks could be a little bit deceiving; she wanted to fit in as much fun as possible. Unless students specifically wanted school credit, math and science were optional. This suited Kelly just fine; she would rather have scrubbed toilets all summer than dealt with math equations. Kelly liked to draw, so she had chosen Introduction to Art History and Studio Arts; it was an added bonus that Andrea, her new favorite teacher, taught both. She was also pleased to discover that Marco the cute professor was her Beginning Italian teacher. She had rounded things out with the History of Ancient Rome, which Dr. Wainwright and Steve were teaching together.

Sheela was busy loading up on notebooks and folders for what seemed to Kelly like dozens of courses. Back home, Sheela only took accelerated classes, and things were no different in Italy: Sheela had approached class selection like a starving person at a buffet. She enrolled in everything from ancient history to volcanology. And instead of a fun elective, she chose Latin.

Sheela consulted a long list. "I still need to swing by a bookstore to pick up some books for Orations."

"What's Orations?"

Sheela smiled. "It's a nerd thing; you wouldn't under-stand. After that, wanna head back? I'm starving."

Kelly collected her pens and notebooks, and threw some colored pencils and a large drawing pad onto her stack, too—sketching in the park seemed like a good way to meet the locals.

"Hey, how about a gelato?" she asked Sheela as she paid for her things. "I still owe you one, remember?"

Sheela grinned. "It's about time. I've been waiting for it since we landed!"

Two gelatos and an hour of people-watching later, Kelly and Sheela dropped their shopping bags on the floor of their room.

"Why is shopping with you so exhausting?" Sheela said, collapsing on her bed.

"When you shop with a master, the pleasure is worth the pain," Kelly replied.

"Not to me. I'm ready to pass out."

Kelly launched a pillow at Sheela's head just as some-one knocked on the door of their suite. She jumped up to answer it, narrowly escaping Sheela's counterattack.

"Hey, babe," Joe said when Kelly opened the door.

Kelly's heart flopped. "Hey yourself."

"Rod and I are hanging out in the lounge, having a little preclass celebration. Wanna join us?"

Kelly shot a glance back at Sheela, who had pointedly

buried her nose in one of her new book purchases. There was no hope for social entertainment there.

Joe nodded toward Sheela. "Do you really want to spend your last night before class watching her study?"

Kelly turned back to Joe with a smile. "What's in it for me?"

"Come and find out. I dare you."

Rodney was playing his guitar when they walked into the lounge. He offered Kelly a water bottle. "Want some?"

Kelly put the bottle to her lips, then put it down again. "Ew, what is this? It smells like turpentine."

Joe laughed. "Grappa. It's great—it'll knock you flat on your ass."

"When you put it that way, it sounds so appealing. I think I'll pass." Kelly curled up on the couch and watched Joe pull a guitar out of its case. "I didn't know you played."

"I guess I'm full of surprises," Joe said.

Joe didn't just play—he was seriously talented. And he and Rod made a good team, improvising and riffing off each other. Kelly shouted out requests, feeling like she had a front-row seat at her own private concert. She was so wrapped up in the music she lost track of time.

It seemed like only minutes later that she was awakened by a hand tussling her hair. "Rise and shine." Joe was kneeling beside her.

Kelly sat up abruptly, instinctively patting her messy hair.

The lights in the lounge had been dimmed and the building was absolutely quiet. "What time is it?"

Joe grinned. "Four."

"Four A.M.?" Kelly cried, shooting off the couch. "Oh, my God! Classes start in four hours."

"Relax," Joe said, rubbing her shoulders. "You slept for a couple of hours down here. You'll be fine."

"I won't be fine. If I wake up Sheela coming into the room, she'll kill me."

"Bore you to death, more like it. Come on, I'll walk you upstairs."

Outside her door, Kelly turned to Joe. "I think I'd better be careful—I have a feeling you could be a bad influence on me."

Joe leaned forward and kissed her lightly on the lips. "Yup, and you're gonna love every minute of it."

Chapter Four

Bleep! Bleep! Bleep! Oh God, not again. Sheela's travel alarm was obviously broken. Kelly peeked at her own clock: 8 A.M.... EIGHT A.M.! She was late for the first day of classes! She was supposed to be in Marco's Italian class right now! Sheela, Minnie, and Lisa were long gone. The least they could have done was wake her up before they left! She jumped out of bed and ran across the hall to the bathroom.

Kelly tore off her T-shirt and shorts and turned on the shower. She'd just rinse off. She didn't have time to wash her hair; she was late enough as it was. She jumped into

the shower and lathered up as fast as she could, which was next to impossible with the freaky shower nozzle. It was on a metal hose that reminded her of the dish rinser in a kitchen sink. To get clean, she had to lather up with one hand while holding the hose in the other hand. She had one side successfully soapy when the hose slipped out of her hand. The nozzle spun around and blasted a shot of water right into her face. So much for having a good hair day. By the time she finished showering, her normally shiny, bouncy hair was limp and stringy.

At least being damp cooled her off for a few minutes. It was too hot in the un-air-conditioned bathroom to blow-dry her hair, so Kelly staggered back to her little room to do her makeup and choose her outfit. She went to grab a top out of her extra suitcase, only to remember that it had been banished to the storage room. She'd been stowing it behind the couch in the common room until one of the little traitors in her suite had complained to the janitor. Now every time Kelly needed something other than the absolute basics, she had to haul her sweaty rear down five flights of stairs, unlock her little cage, and rummage for clothes. It sucked.

She sighed. She had wanted to make a good impression her first day of classes. In fact, last night she had planned to pick out the perfect outfit. Now she'd have to work with whatever she could throw on the fastest.

On top of everything else, she was starving, and the

cafeteria had stopped serving breakfast ages ago. As she picked up her books in the common room, she spied Lisa's jar of organic peanut butter on the table. Kelly looked around nervously and scooped out a big fingerful. It wasn't an Egg McMuffin, but it would keep her from zoning out in Marco's class.

She arrived at Beginning Italian out of breath and already sweaty. So much for the shower. She inched open the classroom door, hoping Marco would be too absorbed in his teaching to take notice. No such luck. He stepped over and swung the door open for her.

"Buon giorno, Signorina Brandt." Marco smiled warmly. "We're so glad you could join us." His smile faded. "I'm always willing to excuse students who are late once. Twice, however, will be a very different story."

"Sorry," Kelly mumbled. With everyone watching, she dragged her sweaty, stringy-haired self to the nearest desk. This was not going to be her day.

That afternoon, Kelly counted her blessings as she emptied her book bag. Her classes had gone well, other than Marco's. And she had loads of time to make up for that. Kelly read a note, written in Sheela's precise script, that was sitting on her pillow. It said she was in the library studying with Jarvis, a boy from her Latin class. The tiny room was all Kelly's! She yawned luxuriously; maybe there was even time to get in a little sunbathing before dinner.

She had just changed out of her sweaty clothes when Lisa appeared in the doorway, her face twisted with rage and an open jar in her hand. Kelly's heart sank. Ever since they'd met, Kelly couldn't so much as blink without kicking off a Lisa lecture: Her makeup was tested on animals, her perfume was too strong, her opinions were superficial or just plain wrong.

"Did you do this?" Lisa demanded, pointing to the gaping crater in the peanut butter.

Kelly nodded. "I missed breakfast this morning and—"

"What kind of person digs their filthy fingers into someone else's food?" Lisa shouted, cutting her off. "Now you've ruined it, and I'll never find another jar here!"

Kelly blinked, taken aback. "At home my friends and I share food all the time. My hands were perfectly clean. And it's not like I double-dipped." Kelly smiled ingratiatingly. "It's one hundred percent spit-free, I promise."

Lisa snorted in exasperation and stormed out of the room, her face as red as a vine-ripened tomato. "And get your dirty towel off the common-room floor!" she shouted. Kelly hung her head guiltily. Caught sticky-handed. She'd just have to avoid Lisa until she cooled off. It was the only way they would both survive the summer in one piece.

Kelly was about to settle in for a catnap when opera music began swelling in the commom room. Minnie had been playing the stuff nonstop, and it sounded to Kelly like a hissy fit set to music. She sighed and stood up. Making friends with Lisa was not going to be an option, but there was still a chance with Minnie. She certainly wouldn't be napping anytime soon; maybe she'd try a little bonding session. She walked into the common room, picking up the towel from her morning rush. Minnie was sitting on the couch with her eyes shut, a blissful smile on her face.

Kelly cleared her throat and Minnie jumped. "Sorry. Mind if I turn it down for a few minutes? I've been wanting to chat with you."

Minnie looked suspicious, but nodded.

Kelly sat down and grabbed a couple of her fashion magazines off the coffee table. "You know, Min, I was thinking you might want to update your wardrobe a bit. Guys like girls who look sophisticated, a little mysterious, even." She started fluffing Minnie's ponytail. "Maybe we could do something to give this hair some body. And I have some mascara that would be perfect for your pale lashes. Those glasses really hide your eyes."

Minnie's lip trembled and she jumped to her feet. "As it happens, I have a boyfriend at home who likes me just the way I am. And I'm very opposed to mascara. It irritates my eyes." She ran into her bedroom, calling over her shoulder, "And don't call me Min!"

The door slammed. So much for trying to be helpful!

Kelly had never felt this way before. When she went to sleepaway camp, it hadn't taken her more than a week to

attract a tight group of friends whom she still kept in touch with. Here, everybody was as eccentric as the plumbing. Her heavy-duty flirting sessions with Joe were fun, but she hadn't really bonded with any girls in the program. This was not acceptable, or understandable. Other than Sheela, she couldn't think of one girl she wanted as a friend.

Kelly headed down to the lounge, hoping to find Joe. He wasn't around, but a few of the jet-set kids were still hanging out. They seemed nice enough—maybe this was her chance to make some new friends.

She turned on her president-of-the-student-council smile, walked over to the group, and sat down. A few of the kids moved over to make room for her on the couch, but otherwise, they were too absorbed in their conversation to pay attention to her. Within two minutes, Kelly realized that they all spoke at least three different languages, interchanging them throughout the conversation. After two minutes more, she realized that even when they spoke English, she didn't have a clue what they were talking about.

"Things haven't been the same since the EU was formed," one girl said.

"*C'est vrai,*" agreed a guy. "It's sucking away every aspect of our national identities. I hope we get to discuss this in Modern International Politics."

"You're taking that?" another girl said. "My friend from Kuala Lumpur took that when she was in the program last year. She said Dr. Wainwright's discussion about the narcissistic culture of American capitalism was fascinating."

Kelly smiled and nodded, feeling like an unsophisticated dolt. Finally she admitted defeat and quietly slunk out of the lounge.

Out in the hall, Kelly took a deep breath. She squared her shoulders and marched out to the terrace like a centurion heading into battle. She was setting herself a goal, right then and there. Kelly was going to find herself a new friend, even if it took the entire week.

To: m&ebrandt@email.com
From: kelcat@email.com
Subject: Please send peanut butter

Dear Mom and Dad,

I can't believe how quickly I'm learning things here—at this rate, I'll be speaking perfect Italian in no time!

The kids here are really interesting—the S.A.S.S. girls and the other PIR students are all American, but they're from every possible background and they come from all over the place. There's also a bunch of kids taking summer classes who go here during the year. A lot of their parents are diplomats—this neighborhood is full of them.

Sheela and I are getting along fine. She's as busy as always and is definitely getting her money's worth here. She's also making a real effort to be more outgoing and

social. Luckily, she's not so popular yet that she can't help me with Italian vocab words—some things never change.

If you see any at the store, can you please send me a jar of organic peanut butter? I want to give it to my room-mate.

I hope you guys are doing well. I miss you like crazy.

LOLXXX,
Kelly

To: kelcat@email.com
From: m&ebrandt@email.com
Subject: Our jet-set daughter

Dear Kel,

Mom and I are so proud of you! I must admit, when you first told us about the program, we were pretty dubious. Now I have no doubts that you're committed, you're moti-vated, and you're going to do great. Who knew that my social butterfly of a daughter was going to turn into a devoted scholar?

Please don't forget to write to your old parents. We miss you, but knowing you're making friends and enjoying your classes makes us very happy.

All my love,
Dad

• • •

Kelly wasn't a morning person to begin with, and she'd stayed up late again with Joe and overslept, as usual. She was positive she'd never learn to speak Italian at the rate she was going. Communicating in a strange language was hard enough when you weren't half-asleep. And Marco, while adorable, was a total hard-ass.

Kelly arrived one measly minute after the clock struck eight. To Marco, she might as well have shown up at eight-thirty.

"Miss Brandt, late again, I see," he said, singling her out before she could make it to her seat.

By now she knew the drill. Sighing, she joined him at the front of the room. Marco paced in front of the blackboard, tossing his black locks and waving a piece of chalk. "Okay, quick-quick, let's conjugate together—*avere*—'to have.' *Io ho*—'I have'…"

Kelly stumbled through the conjugations as the rest of the class looked on. Marco put her through three painful rounds before she was finally allowed to sit down. She tried to ignore the whispers she heard behind her and looked over to Joe for support. He was in his own world, wearing his trademark smirk and doodling in his notebook. Everyone else was diligently parroting away on a new verb, following Marco's chalk like a bouncing ball. It was going to be a major challenge to find anyone friend-worthy in this crew.

Blab, blab, blab. Such a bunch of sheep. And then, it hit her—*the black sheep!* Goth Girl, a.k.a. Marina, was slouched at a desk in the back corner, staring out the window and looking for all the world like she wanted to climb out. Marina would be a perfect person to explore the city with; she was so scary-looking, guys wouldn't dare mess with them. And she *had* to be cool—it took serious guts to dress like a vampire every day.

Marco moved on to *sapere*—"to know." Kelly actually did know this one. She recited along with Marco, a big smile on her face, watching the bouncing chalk with everybody else. Just when this place was starting to get her down, everything was going to fall right into place.

Kelly sat down with Goth Girl at lunchtime. Marina was nose-deep in a book of poems by Allen Ginsberg, which seemed fitting. She was plugged into her iPod and seemed to have no clue Kelly was even there. Finally Kelly worked up the nerve to tap her on the shoulder.

Marina's head popped up and her eyes widened in surprise. She looked Kelly up and down, from her lavender top to her artfully frayed denim miniskirt. Finally, she took off her headphones and spoke. "May I help you?"

She was polite, anyway. Kelly smiled her most electric, appealing smile. "Do you mind if I sit with you?" She was usually the queen of breezy and casual. Where had that slightly desperate edge to her voice come from?

"Suit yourself." Marina returned to her reading.

So Kelly sat there, every bite of her salami sandwich tasting like dirt, watching the minutes crawl by on the clock and straining to think of something to say. It finally came to her.

"Where did you get that nail polish? I've never seen anything like it."

Marina laughed, which seemed encouraging. "Yeah, and you're not likely to." She waved her ragged nails in front of Kelly's face for closer inspection. "My father owns an auto-body shop in Tucson. This is 1974 Buick Electra, Avocado Green."

"It's cool. Um, are you sure it's okay to use that stuff on your nails? They're pretty porous, you know. The chemicals can get absorbed right into your bloodstream. There's a great store in the mall where I used to work that has like every nail polish color under the sun. I bet you could find something just like that. Or maybe mix one up."

"Don't worry yourself. I've already got ink running through my veins." Marina flashed an elaborately tattooed shoulder. Then she shut her book and picked up her spiked leather bag. "See you around, Katie."

Kelly sighed and scooped up her books. In two minutes flat, Marina had reduced her to a dorky, awkward nobody.

Kelly sat in the darkened art-history classroom, watching Andrea's slide show. It wasn't fair that someone as stylish

and together as Andrea was a teacher. Why weren't there any girls like her in the program? She hoped that Andrea's smooth voice would soothe her jangled nerves and wounded pride.

This was one of the few classes in which she felt competent. Statue after statue, all smooth white marble and rippling lines, flickered across the screen. One statue of a young man, in particular, caught Kelly's eye.

"This sculpture is one of the best known in the world," Andrea was saying. "Does anyone know its name?"

Kelly raised her hand. "It's Michelangelo's *David.*"

"Exactly," Andrea said. "Thank you, Kelly."

"A lot of people recognize the statue," Andrea continued. "But very few recognize its unusual proportions." Andrea pointed to the slide. "Look closely at the slide. What do you see?"

Kelly stared at the picture, scanning the statue from head to toe, and then as a whole. She spoke hesitantly. "His head and shoulders are bigger than the rest of his body?"

Andrea smiled. "Good eye, Kelly. Michelangelo designed *David* to be slightly larger at the top. Art historians have several theories about his motives..."

As Andrea talked, Kelly began sketching in her drawing pad. She drew a quick outline of *David*'s body, then started drawing his face, emphasizing his eyes and the curls of his hair. When the lights came back up, she was still drawing away.

"Nice technique." Andrea leaned over her work, studying it carefully. "Do you sketch a lot?"

Kelly shrugged. "I guess so. I like to copy pictures out of magazines."

"Well, keep it up. You have a good grasp of composition and layout. I'd love to see more in studio arts."

Kelly left the classroom beaming. It was, without a doubt, the best thing that had happened to her all week.

Chapter Five

To: tyffaniandco@email.com

From: kelcat@email.com

Subject: Basta!

Dear Tyff,

Now I know why they call Rome the Eternal City—I feel like I've been here an eternity! This place is totally over-whelming.

It's exhausting trying to remember everything here—the

money is different, the language is different, and I don't get the people here at all.

The craziest thing is the way people drive. Cars and scooters come at you from every possible direction. Everybody speeds, changes lanes without looking, and screams at you if you get in their way. Just stepping off the curb you take your life in your hands.

My suite mates and I aren't getting along too well—we're like total opposites. It totally sucks, because we share this tiny room.

I really, really wish you were here. I haven't heard from you for ages—hope you haven't forgotten all about me this summer. Write to me and tell me everything! I can't wait to get out of this place, sleep in my own bed, and spend time with some true friends who actually understand me.

Love you lots,
Kel

Kelly was awakened Saturday morning by a screeching soprano.

"Can you please turn that down?" Kelly yelled to Minnie, pulling the pillow over her head. All she wanted was one more hour of sleep, but the music kept blaring. Kelly sighed and threw her pillow on the floor. There was no going back to sleep now.

She threw open her door and stomped into the common room, where Sheela and Minnie were poring over a thick Italian-history book.

"Do you guys mind?" Kelly said. "It's totally rude to blast music when people are trying to sleep."

"It's past noon, Kelly," Sheela said. "And we have a quiz to study for."

"Isn't that what the library is for?"

Sheela sighed. "You know, you weren't so considerate last night when you woke me up by dropping your shoes on the floor at three A.M."

"I'll take that over these horrible, ear-piercing shrieks anytime," Kelly said.

Minnie opened her mouth like she wanted to say something, then shut it. Her lip started its familiar quivering. "Fine. I'll listen in my room." Once again, Kelly stood in shock as Minnie's door slammed in her face.

"That went well." Sheela sighed and stood up. "I'm going to get some lunch. Do you want to come?"

"I don't understand why you're always taking their side." Despite the scolding she was surely about to get, Kelly was thrilled to finally have Sheela to herself for a little while. Sheela was usually so busy studying with Minnie or Jarvis that seeing her alone was like getting an audience with the pope.

"Siding with them? Please, I feel like I'm being paddled back and forth between the three of you like a Ping-Pong ball. I just don't understand why you go so far out of your way to antagonize them."

This was too much. "Me! I've been patient as a saint with those two nightmares. What did I do?"

"Well, none of us like that you bring Joe back to the room all the time. He's noisy and he's obnoxious. I can't imagine why you're so smitten with him."

Kelly shook her head. "You're being unfair—he's just joking around with you guys. And I don't see how sitting in a public area with a friend makes me antagonistic."

"Okay, then how about the fact that you made Minnie cry again today?"

"That's totally not my fault. She was being a jerk blasting her music. All I did was ask her to turn it down."

Sheela sighed patiently. "Kelly, I'm sure your intentions were good, but last week you told her that her wardrobe stinks, and today you ripped into her beloved opera. You've been a little harsh, don't you think?"

Kelly shrugged. "Well, it's true, isn't it? What self-respecting seventeen-year-old listens to that crap *and* wears flowered shortie overalls? Besides, it takes absolutely nothing to make that girl cry. She's screwed together way too tight." Kelly stabbed little dotted lines into her melon slices with the tines of a fork. "Fine, I'm the devil

incarnate where Minnie is concerned. But what about Lisa? Are you trying to suggest that the reason she hates me is because I bully her, too?"

"I'm not saying you're a bully at all. I'm just saying that if you want to get along with people who are different from you, you're going to have to be a little more considerate. And a lot more tolerant."

Kelly didn't know what Sheela was talking about. At home, she was friendly to everyone. Almost everyone. She at least tried to smile at the socially unfortunate students. You don't get to be president of student council two years running by pissing off the people who voted for you.

"I'm sorry, Sheela, but Lisa is the least tolerant person I've met in my whole life. If you don't eat what she eats, think how she thinks, and do exactly what she says, you get a three-hour lecture."

Sheela laughed. "She is a strong dose. But you have to hand it to her, she's incredibly dedicated to her causes."

Kelly snorted. "Yeah, all four hundred of them. I heard she's organizing a rally in the Piazza del Popolo tomorrow—something about saving the exploited worker bees of the endangered Martian grasslands."

Sheela burst out laughing, a belly-busting, mouth-wide-open laugh. It was music to Kelly's ears, and it sounded a whole lot better than opera.

To: kelcat@email.com

From: tyffaniandco@email.com
Subject: Suite mates . . . who needs 'em?

Dear Kelly,

After everything you did to get to Italy, now you're complaining? (If I could reach you right now, I'd strangle you!)
Anywhere, and anything, has to be better than this stag-
nant social backwater! Believe me, you've so got the better end of the bargain. Your suite mates are just jealous of
your divine fashion sense, that's all. Blow them off, and
have some fun!

Love you,

Tyff

Kelly met Joe down in the lounge for movie night that
evening. She neatly avoided Lisa and Minnie, who both
glared at her, and settled down on a couch next to Joe.
Scoping the room, she noticed that Sheela was sitting with
Jarvis, deep in conversation.

"Look at the lovebirds," Joe cracked. "How sweet."

"It is, actually," Kelly said. "He's the perfect kind of guy
to get Sheela out of her shell—you know, bookish, and not
intimidating."

Joe smirked. "Translation: The guy's lame."

"Whatever," Kelly said. "If she's happy, I'm happy."

The movie flickered onto the screen. It was hard to concentrate with Joe playing with her hair and whispering in

her ear. Kelly looked up and caught Sheela glaring at them. Guiltily, she shushed Joe. Sheela and Joe were both important to Kelly, and she wanted them to get along. But she was starting to think that only a diplomat could make that happen.

Chapter Six

1. Go to bed earlier.
2. Write home more.
3. Make nice with the suite mates.
4. Practice your Italian—in public!
5. Finish your reading assignments—EVERY NIGHT!!!
6. Try to be happy!!!!!

Kelly sat under a shady tree in the school courtyard Sunday morning, making a list in her notebook. She was

tired of trying to break into the tight clique of day-schoolers in the cafeteria, and the nerdy program kids bored her. Joe didn't "do" breakfast, and even if he did, Kelly knew it would take a crowbar to get him out of bed before 10 A.M. Recently, she had taken to bringing her yogurt and coffee outside every morning. Goth Girl was sitting on a bench nearby, and glanced up from her book to give Kelly a mock salute.

It didn't matter. In the two and a half weeks she'd been in Italy, this was the first time Kelly was truly excited about something. At dinner the night before, Dr. Wainwright had announced that whoever was interested could join him for a trip to the shore.

"Lido di Ostia is not the prettiest beach in the world, but I love it for two reasons. First, it's only a half hour away on the metro. Second, Ostia Antica was the major seaport of ancient Rome and its base of naval operations during the heyday of the empire. Where else in the world can you find a festive seaside resort sitting cheek by jowl with some pretty spectacular Roman ruins?

"We'll get in a little history and still have plenty of time to soak up some rays. And I promise I won't wear my Speedo." Dr. Wainwright had guffawed.

Kelly had smiled over at Joe, who gave her a big wink and the "hang loose" sign.

The group was leaving right after breakfast, so Kelly hustled down to her storage bin to grab the new black bikini she'd bought especially for this summer. With her

64

mom's voice echoing in her ears, she grabbed sunscreen and her straw hat. Then she bolted up the five flights to her room to grab a couple of her reading assignments and the fashion magazine Starr had just sent her.

Lido di Ostia was a bit seedy and run-down, but there were loads of pizzerias, bars, and seafood restaurants scattered along the beach, along with some old-timey hotels that needed a paint job. The group staked out a patch of sand and spread out their towels. Kelly settled back to people-watch. Big Italian grandmas romped in the surf with toddlers beside young couples in skimpy bathing suits. Families laid out elaborate picnic lunches, complete with wine, on their beach blankets. One thing she could say for sure: Italians knew how to eat.

Wonder of wonders, Sheela had actually come on the trip. She had been on the fence all morning, and it took serious coaxing from Kelly to get her on the metro. She was about as scantily dressed as Kelly had seen her in years—normal-length shorts and a properly fitting T-shirt, with a bathing suit peeking out underneath. Sheela had sexy, womanly curves that other girls would have loved to show off. But back home, while Kelly's other friends casually strutted around the locker room in thongs, Sheela cringed if anyone caught even a glimpse of her bra. Kelly was glad to see her loosening up a little.

Best of all, Sheela was sitting with Jarvis again. The two

of them were talking up a storm, and the way Sheela was laughing and leaning forward was unmistakable—in her own quiet way, she was flirting! The little devil knew how to have fun, after all. Kelly felt strangely proud of her—she had learned from the master. Maybe Kelly would take her aside and give her a few extra pointers later.

Kelly pulled out her sketch pad and scanned the beach for a subject. Andrea was walking toward her, a pair of to-die-for sandals on her pedicured feet. Kelly wondered where she'd bought them.

"Hey, Kelly," Andrea said. "I'm glad to see you brought your sketch pad. Does that mean you're working on the assignment that was due Friday?"

Kelly's heart was hammering. How could she have forgotten? Andrea had asked the art-history students to choose a building or person of historical significance to Rome and do a rendering in charcoal. The class was only held Tuesdays and Thursdays, but Andrea wanted the kids to have as much time as possible to work on their drawings. So she'd given them until Friday afternoon to hand them in. Kelly had completely spaced out; she hadn't even decided on a subject, let alone started sketching.

Andrea leaned forward to look at the open page of Kelly's drawing pad. A lone seagull, drawn in pencil, soared across the page.

"That's lovely," Andrea said, "but not quite the historical subject I was looking for."

Kelly blushed. "Andrea, I'm so sorry. I completely forgot. May I please have until tomorrow to get it to you?"

Andrea looked at Kelly for a long moment, then sighed. "Tomorrow morning, eight A.M."

Kelly brightened. "Thank you so much! I'll get started on it right away!"

Andrea nodded. "I've heard you've been late to several classes recently. If you're soaking up all of the wonderful opportunities that Italy has to offer, that's great, but please keep in mind that you're here to learn, too. You have too much talent to let it go to waste."

"I'll try harder, Andrea," Kelly said, flipping to a fresh page to begin her drawing assignment. "I promise."

Kelly watched Andrea head down the beach. Then she turned back to her sketch pad, thinking. She had some serious work to do, and not a whole lot of time.

Later on, they were going to visit the ruins of Lido di Ostia's forum. She'd definitely be able to start a drawing then, and snap some digital photos as well. She could put the finishing touches on it after dinner. She'd stay up as late as she needed to.

"What up, Brandt?" The voice was right in her ear, and it scared her silly.

She gave Joe a playful poke in the ribs. "Where did you sneak up from?"

"Rod and I are chillin' farther down the beach. This place blows, man. There's not a wave to be caught." Joe

put his arm around Kelly's shoulders. "If you weren't here in that bikini, the trip would be a total waste."

Kelly finally had a chance to check out the tattoo on his arm—it was a band of bright blue waves, with foamy whitecaps on top. She noticed that Joe's blue-green eyes looked a little glassy.

"Are you high?"

He laughed. "Maybe a little bit. Rod and I hooked up with a guy in Ostiense last night and scored some decent weed. We just fired one up. You want some? There's a delightfully private alley just across the highway."

"Not for me, thanks. Anyway, I'm happy to watch the seagulls. God, have you ever seen such a bunch of stiffs in your life? I can't believe Dr. W got them out of the library for a whole afternoon. I bet kids in Malibu aren't allowed to be this pasty."

Joe didn't seem to be listening to her. He looked around furtively. "Wanna see something?" He took her hand and slid a warm piece of metal into her palm.

"Thrilling. A key."

"Not just any key, babe. This is the front-door key to the PIR. With this miraculous item in my possession, curfew means nothing to me."

"Where did you get this?"

"I'm tricky that way. Let's just say I'm real good at getting what I want." He gazed at her meaningfully. "After dinner tonight, I'm going to take you dancing. How about it?"

Kelly's heart leaped, but then she hesitated. "I really shouldn't. I have to finish an assignment for Andrea's class. It's already late."

Joe snorted. "It's not due *today,* is it?"

"Well, no, but—"

"So finish it tomorrow morning." He smiled at her. "You know you're dying to check out the club scene here."

What could Kelly say? What Joe Leahy wanted, Joe Leahy got.

"I'll be there," she said.

Joe took her to Testaccio, the neighborhood right next to Aventino. It was a pretty grim-looking area, kind of industrial and blah. "Some of the hottest clubs in the city are here," Joe told her. "Rod and I scouted out a whole bunch of 'em."

Dr. Wainwright had already taken them to Testaccio for an ancient-history class. Back in ancient times, it was the city dump. Later on, it became the part of town where all the city's slaughterhouses were located. Kelly was relieved to know they were long gone.

One of the highlights of the neighborhood was a pyramid where some big-shot politician was buried a couple thousand years ago. Kelly was kind of shocked to see a pyramid in the middle of Rome, but it turned out that the ancient Romans were totally crazy for Egyptian stuff.

The area was hopping with young people heading out to

eat or party. Joe obviously knew exactly where he was going, and grabbing her hand, he led her into a nondescript old warehouse building. Inside, strobes popped like crazy and techno pulsed so loudly she could feel it in her gut. Kelly's heart pounded with excitement. Why on earth hadn't she had a real date with Joe sooner?

"C'mon, let's get a drink." They worked their way toward the bar.

One of her parents' conditions for Kelly attending the PIR was that she sign a contract specifically geared toward Rome. Kelly went through its conditions in her mind.

I, Kelly Rebecca Brandt, agree to obey the following terms for the duration of my time in Italy. I understand that failure to comply with these rules will result in immediate removal from the program:

1. No alcohol except wine, and only at supervised school functions.
2. No drugs other than medication prescribed by a doctor to treat a specific illness.
3. No piercings or tattoos!
4. I will not ride scooters, Vespas, or motorcycles, either as a driver or a passenger.
5. I will finish all daily schoolwork before pursuing leisure activities.

6. I will not go out by myself at night.

7. I will call or e-mail home at least once a week.

No alcohol except wine, and only at supervised school functions. There was no way to get around that one, so she decided that bending the rules halfway was her best bet.

"I'll just have a glass of wine."

Joe waved his hand dismissively. "Nah, you're in Rome, babe! You've gotta try something really Italian tonight." He waved over the bartender and shouted in his ear. *"Due Campari soda, per favore."* He handed her a glass of what looked like a Shirley Temple. "Drink up, Brandt. We have serious dancing to do."

Kelly put the glass to her lips and nearly gagged. "You're joking, right? This stuff is utterly foul!"

Joe laughed. "Tastes like cough medicine, right? But Italians love it. They're really into the bitter taste. Drink up—the farther down you get, the more you'll like it."

They were out on the dance floor for hours, having a blast. Kelly did feel a twinge of guilt about lying to Sheela; Kelly had told her that she was hanging out in Joe and Rodney's room and wouldn't be back until late.

Right now Sheela was probably in the library with Jarvis, grinding away at her Latin. Kelly probably should have been there, too, working on her art assignment. She'd get up early tomorrow to finish it, but drawing bleary-eyed seemed like a bad way to try to get back into Andrea's

good graces. She'd just have to work harder on her next project.

"You still have that key, right?" Kelly shouted over the music.

Joe pulled a string out from under his shirt and dangled the key in front of her face. "No worries at all, babe. Dr. Wainwright locks the door at one A.M., but he never does a room check. We can stay out as long as we want. Just relax and have fun. You seem like you need it." He leaned in and gave her a light kiss on the lips.

Kelly shut her eyes and smiled. The music washed over her like the turquoise waves of the Mediterranean Sea.

Kelly giggled as she struggled to open the door to her suite. Joe was leaning against the door, blocking the keyhole and laughing loudly.

"Come on, Joe. Let me go to bed," she said for about the fourth time. "It's three, and I can't be late for class tomorrow."

Joe laughed even louder, a sloppy grin spreading across his face. "Why break your perfect record? If you showed up on time, people would freak."

Kelly gave him a playful shove. Joe had sucked down about three too many Camparis at the club, leaving Kelly to track down a taxi while he dozed on the curb. When they finally got back to the dorm, she almost had to carry him upstairs. If she'd had more than one drink herself, they might still be in Testaccio.

Joe nuzzled her neck. "Let's go down to the lounge and crash on the couch for a while."

"Yeah, right." Kelly rolled her eyes. This had been fun for about the first five minutes, but now it was getting ridiculous. All Kelly wanted to do was go to sleep. "Just because they don't do room checks doesn't mean that we won't wake everybody with all the noise we're making. My roommates would love to see me get busted." She ducked under his arm and triumphantly turned the key in the lock. "Say good night, Joe," she said, giving him a quick peck on the cheek as she squeezed through her half-open door.

"Good night, Joe!" he yelled after her.

She could still hear him laughing and stumbling down the hallway as she shut the door and slid off her shoes. Then the overhead light switched on.

"Don't bother trying to be quiet now," a steely voice said from behind her. "We're all wide-awake."

Kelly turned from the door to find Sheela, Lisa, and Minnie all standing in the common room, looking disheveled and, even worse, incredibly grumpy.

"I'm so sorry, you guys," Kelly said, giggling nervously. "We lost track of time and—"

"Save it," Lisa muttered. "The least you could have done

was dump him in his room first so we'd be spared the drunken drama."

Sheela sighed. "Since it's too late for that, why don't we all try to go back to sleep?"

Kelly looked into three sleepy, glowering faces. She wanted to say she was sorry again, but there didn't seem to be much point. Not at three in the morning, anyway. She picked up her shoes and, head hanging, headed off to bed.

Chapter Seven

The morning of the program's trip to the Vatican, Kelly overslept yet again. She and Joe had gone out together almost every night for the last two weeks, and last night had been no exception. Kelly was so pumped up that she didn't mind the sweltering temperature in her little room. Even Andrea's reprimand, for handing in her art project another day late, couldn't dampen her mood.

While she showered, her mind replayed the highlights of the evening before: She and Joe had hung out on the terrace until the small hours, talking, laughing, and kissing. She was still smiling as she swiped on a little mascara and

grabbed the first clean outfit in her drawer, pink cargo shorts and a yellow tank top.

She and Joe exchanged sly grins as she bounded up to the group already assembled in front of the school building. He didn't look any the worse for wear, she noticed. Hopefully she didn't, either. Andrea was standing at the head of the crowd, impeccable as usual, waiting for them to quiet down. Kelly felt her cool gaze sweep up and down over her outfit. She fixed Andrea with her sweetest, most innocent smile and mouthed, "Sorry I'm late." Andrea nodded curtly and led the group down the street, where a pair of vans waited to take them to the Vatican City.

To Kelly's surprise, Andrea motioned for Joe to get on the bus first and sat down next to him. Kelly plopped down a few rows behind. She looked around for Sheela and saw her climbing the steps into the other van, a notebook tucked under her arm.

As they began the usual bob and weave through traffic, Andrea gave them a little background on the day's activities. They'd check out St. Peter's Square, go into the Basilica, and spend several hours in the Vatican museums, ending up at the Sistine Chapel. Apparently, the Basilica was the largest cathedral in the world, and the *Pietà*, by Michelangelo, was one of the many great treasures they were going to see. Andrea's tone became reverent as she described the painstaking restoration of the frescoes in the Sistine Chapel. Michelangelo's ceiling, one of the most recognizable artworks in the world, was first to be cleaned. When it was completed, Michelangelo's original, vibrant palette was visible for the first time in centuries. Seeing it in this condition was a privilege that generations of visitors had missed out on.

Kelly let Andrea's voice wash over her. Andrea was a great speaker, and it was obvious to Kelly that she never got tired of sharing her vast knowledge. Even on three hours' sleep, Kelly could feel herself getting caught up in Andrea's enthusiasm.

Soon the imposing dome of the Vatican loomed ahead, and they followed Andrea and Steve to the giant Egyptian obelisk standing in the center of St. Peter's Square. Kelly felt tiny in this enormous space, with thousands of tourists and hundreds of years of history surrounding her. Andrea continued her speech over the bubbling of two gigantic fountains situated on either side of the piazza.

"We have now entered a state that does not belong to Rome. The Vatican City is governed entirely by its own laws—it has its own police force, post office, money, and even its own radio station.

"The earliest buildings date back to the mid-fifteenth century, and many of the greatest Italian artists of all time were involved in its design and decoration. The Vatican Museums, which we'll visit this morning, contain an incredible array of treasures of immeasurable value. You will see magnificent examples of mosaic, tapestries,

ceramics, metalwork—pretty much every medium imagi-nable, all created by master artists and craftsmen and spanning many eras, right up to our own."

Andrea went on to rattle off a list of artists, whose names, Kelly noticed with some irritation, Sheela dutifully wrote down. Kelly knew Michelangelo, obviously, and Raphael and Bernini sounded familiar, but the others meant nothing to her. She watched some birds picking at a piece of bread on the ground and wished she had had time to eat some breakfast.

A change in Andrea's voice got her attention. "Whatever your religious beliefs, it's hard to visit this little city-state without being moved by what you see. It is also impossible to enjoy its riches if you don't respect the beliefs of those who live and work here. If you read your trip notes last night, you will know that as we prepare to enter the Basilica, you must be dressed appropriately. Shoulders and legs must be covered." She looked straight at Kelly. "Otherwise, the Swiss Guard will prevent you from enter-ing the Vatican buildings." She motioned toward two men standing at attention on either side of the Basilica's entrance. Their brightly striped outfits made them look like court jesters, but judging from their stern faces and the big ax each held, they meant business.

A knot formed in the pit of Kelly's stomach as she watched several girls untie long-sleeve shirts from around their waists and put them on over their tank tops. And they weren't wearing shorts or flip-flops, either. This place had its own laws—who knew what would happen to violators? Kelly's eyes darted around the square, looking for a souvenir shop where she could buy something, anything, to wear inside. Behind her, a couple of other group members began to whisper. Kelly usually enjoyed being the center of attention, but at the moment she wanted to curl into a ball right there on the cobblestones.

Andrea and Steve began to shepherd the group in the direction of the Basilica. As they left, Andrea glanced over her shoulder at Kelly, not entirely unkindly. "We'll take a lunch break in a few hours. Why don't you go change and meet up with us back here at one P.M.?"

Kelly nodded, too mortified to speak. As she stood watching her classmates head off to the cathedral, Joe turned back and winked broadly, a huge smile on his face. She felt like smacking him—he thought this was funny? Why the hell hadn't he warned her? Sheela kept her head down, seemingly absorbed in her notes. She hadn't looked at Kelly once.

"Idiot!" Kelly paced through St. Peter's Square, blinking back tears and trying to guess the direction of the nearest metro station. Every slap of her flip-flops on the stones pounded in her ears like a gunshot. Rows of majestic statues stared down at her from the curving walls of the Vatican; even they seemed to disapprove.

She had really, really screwed up this time. It was bad enough that she was breaking curfew almost every night and showing up late for class almost daily, but to not read the instructions and to show such disrespect in a holy place! Even Joe had taken five minutes to read the fact sheets.

Kelly felt like puking. Sheela was right for lecturing her all the time; she had worked so hard to get here, to earn her parents' trust, and all she had done lately was act like a jerk. Andrea was sure to tell Dr. Wainwright about this, and she'd probably mention all the times Kelly had fallen asleep in class, too. She wondered if she'd be sent home.

Kelly gazed absently into the huge fountain that Andrea mentioned was designed by an artist named, fittingly, Fontana. She took a deep breath and let it out slowly. It was nine-thirty; more than three hours until the group came back for lunch. Shopping on Via del Corso crossed her mind, but Kelly reluctantly pushed away temptation. Maybe she could still salvage something from this disaster. When life gives you lemons, make *limonata*.

She turned slowly in a circle, scanning the piazza until she saw a tourist information office. She entered timidly, halfway expecting to be thrown out, but the cute young man at the desk couldn't have been kinder or more sympathetic. And he spoke perfect English. He told her exactly how to get to the metro station, which ticket to buy, and how to find her stop. Kelly glanced at his name badge:

LUIGI. Kelly thanked him and headed off toward Via Ottaviano with a new sense of purpose. Starting now, she'd prove that she deserved to be in Italy, do nothing else to piss off her teachers, and never blow off an assignment again.

A half hour later, Kelly was back on the familiar streets of Aventino. She stopped at the local pastry shop for a latte and a *pane cioccolato*—sugar and caffeine to fuel her journey. Up in her room, Kelly put on a pair of light gray pants, a gauzy, long-sleeve blouse, and a pair of black flats. She pulled her hair into a ponytail. Then she tucked the fact sheets, her sketchbook, and a couple of pencils into her bag and retraced her path to the metro.

When she stepped back through the doors of the Vatican tourist office, Luigi beamed at her. *"Perfetto!"* He had a really sweet smile.

"*Grazie.* I have about an hour and a half before I meet my group. Is there a short tour I can take?"

Luigi produced a small booklet and slid it over the counter. "Well, a day and a half would be better, but such is life. There are three tours, and this is the shortest one." He circled something in the book. "Here." He scribbled a note on a piece of official-looking stationery. "The line at this hour is way too long. Your friends will be gone by the time you get to the chapel. Instead, take the little bus that stops right out front. It will leave you at the side entrance

of the galleries. Give this note to the guards, and they will make sure that you get inside with enough time to catch up with your group and see some masterpieces, too.

"Perhaps your friends will be persuaded to come back with you another time and you can come and visit me again. But now you must run and enjoy the *musei. Arrivederci, signorina.*"

Kelly plunked down a hefty sum for a detailed Vatican guide, thanked Luigi for the umpteenth time, and trotted off toward the bus stop. She had always enjoyed making art more than looking at it. Museums were exhausting; there was always more information than she could process. But today, if only to please Andrea, she was determined to soak up as much culture as possible.

Kelly was lucky in one respect; thanks to Luigi's VIP treatment, she made it to the special entrance and got through security with just over an hour remaining. The first gallery alone made Kelly's head spin; the popes lived like royalty, and every inch of this place seemed to be covered in intricate gilding, lush tapestries, and marble. The other visitors milled around at a snail's pace, plugged into their audio guides, shuffling from one masterpiece to the next. Kelly weaved through them like a Vespa in traffic, trying not to mow down any innocent obstacles in her path.

By twelve-thirty, she had made her way through a labyrinth of salons, and knew the difference between a fresco and a relief. It seemed that every famous episode in the Bible had been illustrated for the Catholic Church by one Renaissance luminary after another. Raphael, check. Caravaggio, check. Michelangelo, all over the place. Her head sweeping from side to side, Kelly made mental notes that she planned to write down as soon as she had the opportunity.

The rest of her group finally came into view as she puffed her way into the Sistine Chapel. Andrea was whispering animatedly, sweeping her arms skyward to point out details in each of the elaborate panels that lined the ceiling. In the center, Kelly could see the renowned image of God creating Adam, their hands outstretched and fingers touching. Other visitors to the chapel casually circled Andrea, trying to overhear her commentary on the frescoes, some peering up at the ceiling through binoculars. When Andrea saw Kelly, she gave her an approving nod. "Glad you made it back."

Kelly tipped her head back until she got dizzy, listening to Andrea's story of how the pope had asked Michelangelo, who considered himself a sculptor, to paint the chapel ceiling. Michelangelo worked day and night for four years, under constant pressure to finish the work, until his eyes went bad. She told them how, after the frescoes were completed, Pope Paul III had brought in another artist to paint clothing on some of the naked figures. It

wasn't until the 1990s, when the frescoes were cleaned and restored, that those clothes were removed, revealing Michelangelo's work just as he created it.

As they stepped out of the museum into the bright sunlight, Kelly could see how energized Andrea was. She beamed at the class, her eyes shining and her cheeks flushed.

Steve met the group in front of the galleries to take over from Andrea for the rest of the day. "Okay, crew," he said. "Let's go explore an even more important Italian art form— lunch!"

When she returned to her room after dinner, Kelly got busy studying the book she had bought from Luigi. She was lying on the lumpy couch, browsing through its pages, when Sheela came stomping in.

"Get your feet off the sofa. It's not yours."

Kelly sat up quickly, brushing at the fabric with her book. "What bee flew up your butt? Are you pissed off that I missed the museums today? I caught up, and I'm gonna read this book from cover to cover. Andrea will hardly be able to tell that I wasn't there with you guys. And what do you care, anyway?"

"Are you serious?" Sheela threw her bag over the back of her desk chair and began emptying it noisily. Despite her friend's foul mood, Kelly had to suppress a smile;

Sheela crammed more junk into her bag than could fit into the average one-bedroom apartment.

Sheela put her face up close to Kelly's, her dark eyes throwing off sparks. "Dr. Wainwright is a friend of my family. Since you were wait-listed at S.A.S.S., he was probably reluctant to accept you into the Programma at all. We've only been here a few weeks, and already you've hooked up with the class slacker, gone out of your way to learn absolutely nothing, and showed up at the Vatican in freaking hot pants! Every immature, irresponsible thing you do is a bad reflection on me."

Kelly was her father's daughter. How would a lawyer argue this case? She paused to compose herself. "First of all, they're not hot pants. They're cargo shorts. Second, I'm my own person; I certainly don't think anyone is confusing me with you. And you know, you might have warned me about the clothing thing."

"And when would I have done that?" Sheela's voice was really rising now. "After dinner, when you ran off to party with Joe? When you came stomping into the bedroom at four A.M., giggling? Or perhaps this morning, when you slept through not only my alarm, but yours, too. Both times it went off. So typical of you to think that what happened today is anybody's fault but your own."

Kelly sank deeper into the couch. Perhaps the best defense wasn't a good offense, after all. She had never

seen Sheela so furious. Even if she didn't rat her out to Dr. Wainwright, Sheela could do even more damage by telling Kelly's parents.

"I'm sick of this, Kelly. I'm sick of feeling embarrassed for you, and I'm so sick of making excuses for your crappy behavior. This is exactly what I was afraid would happen if you came here."

With much effort, Sheela hiked her bag back over her shoulder and walked to the door. "I didn't travel four thousand miles to watch you screw up and ruin everybody else's summer. Do me a favor—from now on, whatever you choose to do, do it without me."

Kelly stared at the computer screen for the longest time, her eyes prickling with tears. She was getting nowhere with her homework. She was dying for a BLT, a Fluffernutter, or anything that wasn't pasta and didn't have olive oil in it. She was starting to fantasize about finding a little pensione somewhere, with fluffy pillows like she had at home and lots and lots of extra-icy air-conditioning.

She had thought that catching up to the group would make everything okay, but Sheela was so pissed anyway that Kelly might as well have blown off the trip entirely and gone shopping. Worst of all, while she was sitting in the bathtub that morning trying to shave her legs, she had overheard two girls, whose voices she didn't recognize, talking about her.

"She completely embarrassed herself yesterday. Minnie says she's a total brat—she acts all superior, and keeps borrowing their stuff all the time without asking. And don't even get me started on her fling with that loser Joe—I don't know what that girl is thinking."

"She's not thinking, obviously. And poor Sheela. They know each other from home or something—I guess that's why she feels like she has to apologize for Kelly all the time."

For the second time in as many days, Kelly felt utterly humiliated. She put down her razor—she was too upset to maneuver it safely—and sat in the tub until she was certain the girls had left. Then she got dressed and went down to Joe's room. But instead of being sympathetic, he almost ruptured himself laughing.

"I'm sorry, babe, but it was so freakin' funny yesterday— you should have seen the look on your face. I can't believe you blew off the reading assignment—it was only like two pages long." Joe playfully ran a finger down her cheek. "If only I had been in your room to help you get dressed, this never would have happened."

Kelly swatted his hand away. "It's not funny, Joe! I made a deal with my parents that if they let me come here, I wouldn't do anything to disappoint them. Sheela knows that we've been breaking curfew and drinking. She could totally get me sent home. What if we chilled for a couple of weeks? We can still go out, but maybe just on the week-

ends, and maybe we can get back before Dr. W locks the door."

Joe looked at her through his blond curls and shot her a killer smile. "I think that's what your boring friend Sheela would do." He put his arms around her and pulled her close. "You're making way too big a thing of this. You're in Italy, it's summertime, and you're seventeen years old. You need to relax." He stroked her hair and kissed her on the forehead.

And she did relax. At least until she got back to her room that night and faced Sheela's unyielding silence.

Chapter Eight

Kelly had spent all of Saturday morning crying. She was so distraught that even Lisa took pity on her, bringing a completely nonvegan breakfast up to the room for her.

Grandma's locket was gone. Kelly had promised her mother she'd never take it off, and she hadn't—she'd worn it the night before when she went clubbing.

Kelly hadn't noticed that it was missing until morning. The first thing she had done was run out into the common room, where she had quietly undressed at the crack of dawn so as not to disturb Sheela. She searched the bathroom, the stairwells, even the driveway, praying it would

turn up. The thought of telling her parents it was gone made Kelly sick.

Even though she was still angry, Sheela tried to come in and talk to her. But Kelly was in no mood for reconciliation and she couldn't bear to be comforted. How could she have been so careless?

There was a quiet tap at her door. "Go away, Sheela!"

"It's not Sheela, it's me." Joe stepped in and sat down on her bed. "I hear you're having a tough day." He massaged her shoulders and she felt herself starting to relax a little.

"I really screwed up this time. I can't believe I lost the locket. My mother will never forgive me—it was my grand-mother's most prized possession." A tear slid down Kelly's cheek. "I should just go home and face my punishment."

"I won't let you go home. You're the smartest and pret-tiest girl in the building. Except for Signora Peretti, maybe."

Despite herself, Kelly laughed.

"Sitting here crying all day isn't gonna bring your neck-lace back." Joe brushed a tear off her cheek. "Come down-stairs and have some dinner with me. You probably haven't eaten anything today, right? After that, I'm going to take you out and I absolutely guarantee you that we'll have a good time."

Kelly shook her head. "You go without me. I'm not hun-gry."

"Are you sure?"

Kelly nodded.

"All right." Joe stood up. "After I get back from dinner, you're all mine."

Kelly and Joe went to a new place in Ostiense. The club had an ultrachic, exotic vibe, with dim lighting and swags of bright, embroidered fabric covering the walls and ceilings. Little tentlike alcoves stuffed with mirrored pillows circled the dance floor and the scent of incense hung in the air. Kelly couldn't help but cheer up as she and Joe made their grand entrance, hand in hand.

As they pressed their way through the crowd, Joe waved to someone sitting in a corner booth. It was Rodney, Joe's roommate, with a girl Kelly had never seen before. "This place is hot, man! I can't believe we didn't come here sooner," Rodney said. "This is Laura." The cute, dark-haired girl with him smiled nervously. Apparently she didn't speak much English.

"Who wants a drink?" Rod asked.

"I've been thinking all day about how to make Kelly forget her troubles and have some fun," Joe said, giving Rodney a meaningful look. "Excuse us a minute, ladies, we'll be back in no time."

Both guys took off, leaving Kelly with Laura. She seemed sweet, but she was as nervous speaking English as Kelly was speaking Italian. Finally, Kelly decided to try the universal language—fashion. Using elaborate hand gestures, she managed to compliment Laura on her dress. The girls

were conversing in an animated combination of English, Italian, and mime when the boys returned.

"This is the house specialty," Joe said, handing her a stemmed glass. "Blood-orange juice and *prosecco.*" Kelly took a sip. It was much better than Campari; it tasted like champagne and orange juice to her, but it was a beautiful pink color. A few sips later, she found herself laughing and loosening up. Laura seemed to like it, too; she drained her glass in record time and asked Rodney to get her another.

Kelly wasn't even halfway through her own drink before she started feeling strange. The lights seemed to dim, and her head was pounding. She looked over at Laura, who had a bewildered look on her face.

Kelly had a sudden, overwhelming urge to lie down in the pile of pillows and nap. Joe and Rodney were still on their feet, swaying to the house music blasting through the room. But behind her, Laura had curled up on the banquette, moaning quietly as if she were in pain. Even in her groggy state, Kelly could tell that Laura was in far worse shape than she was. She reached out and rubbed the girl's back comfortingly.

What was going on?

Finally it dawned on her. Laying both hands on the table in front of her, Kelly worked her way to a standing position. She grabbed Joe by the front of his shirt and screamed in his ear.

"You bastard! What did you put in the drinks?" She pounded his chest with her fists. Her voice sounded funny in her ears.

"Relax, babe, relax. It was just something to take you out of yourself for a while. I only gave you each a little bit. It'll wear off soon. Just chill." He squinted past her at Laura, then turned to Rodney.

"Yo, Rod! We've got to get your girl out of here. She's not looking too good." Joe's own face looked gray, and his shirt was wet with sweat. Rodney was still grooving, his eyes shut, completely oblivious to what was going on.

"Listen, Kelly. We've got to take Laura home." He gently pushed her back into her seat. "Sit tight and I'll come back for you." He bent down and hoisted Laura onto her feet. She groaned, but put her arm around his shoulder. Rodney, who had finally gotten a clue, took the other side, and the three of them stumbled off into the crowd.

Kelly sat for what seemed like hours, her head in her hands. She was desperately thirsty, and somehow managed to get someone to bring her a big glass of water. A couple of times, men came over to her and said things she didn't understand. "Don't touch me!" she shrieked, and they retreated. She had to get out of there. She picked her way back through the crowd until she found the door.

"*Taxi, per favore. Emergencia.*" She wasn't sure what was the right word. But the bouncer seemed to know what she

meant and flipped open his cell phone. She counted every second until a little white car pulled up in front and the bouncer helped her in.

Kelly opened the windows all the way. The cabbie's driving, which verged on homicidal, was making her nauseous. When they arrived at the school gates, he peeled off without even waiting for her to get inside safely.

Kelly stood alone on the gravel driveway, shaking and struggling to catch her breath. Her limbs felt like overcooked linguini. The front door was locked; she was dressed to the teeth, exhausted and disheveled. She looked at her tiny evening purse in despair. Why hadn't she carried a bag big enough to hold her cell phone? If she could only reach her, Kelly was pretty sure Sheela would come down to let her in. She'd be furious, but what else was new? The nearest pay phone was several blocks away, on a dark, deserted street; Kelly didn't feel like taking any more risks tonight.

A strange feeling of calm came over her. This was it. It was over. She would be sent home. Sheela could have the perfect summer she deserved, once Kelly was out of the way. Suddenly she understood why Andrea had kept her apart from Joe the morning of the Vatican trip; it was clear to everybody but Kelly that he was bad news.

Andrea. Kelly wrapped her shawl tightly around her shoulders and walked around the side of the main build-

94

ing to the small annex of apartments where the instructors lived.

Andrea didn't say a word when she answered the door; she just looked Kelly up and down, from her smudged face to her strappy, metallic sandals, then led her to the couch.

"Are you okay?" Andrea sat cross-legged next to her, watching her closely. "Are you hurt?"

Kelly shook her head. "I'm sorry to disturb you so late. I didn't know what else to do."

"It's all right. Part of my job is to be here when you guys need me. And I have a front-door key, so unless you wanted to sleep out on the steps, it was a good idea to knock. You know that you missed curfew by more than an hour, right?"

Kelly nodded, blushing. "I had a really horrible day. A few friends took me dancing to try and cheer me up, but we got separated. I spent a long time trying to find them, until I realized that it was almost one. So I called a cab and came back by myself." She looked down at the rug. "My Italian sucks, so I got pretty scared. I guess I just panicked."

Kelly was certain that Andrea had never, ever done anything so stupid in her entire life. Even without makeup, she looked glamorous and put-together.

Andrea watched her face closely. "That's a believable

story, but I don't entirely buy it. When you knocked on my door, you looked absolutely terrified. Are you sure there's nothing else you want to tell me about tonight? Maybe who you were with?"

"I'd rather not, if that's okay."

"Well, I can't force you to. Though Marco is pretty sure he saw you at a club last week with Joe Leahy."

Kelly stared down at the rug, saying nothing.

Andrea paused carefully. "Were you drinking?"

"I only had about half a drink. Something pink and fizzy. It made me feel kind of sick, so I didn't finish it." Always answer the question honestly, but don't offer any extra information. That's what her father always said.

"Listen, Kelly, being here is a big adjustment for a girl your age. Having so much freedom can make somebody a little crazy if they're not used to it, and sometimes it's pretty easy to forget the rules." She gazed at Kelly with clear gray eyes. "I know you've been having a tough time concentrating recently. Does whatever upset you earlier relate to that?"

Kelly looked down at the twisted tissue in her hands. "No, nothing like that. This was something brand-new, and like everything else, it was all my fault. I understand why everybody here hates me." She swallowed the sob that was rising in her chest; the last thing she wanted was for Andrea to see her cry.

"Look, recognizing that you need to be more responsible is an important first step to changing things for the better. As for everyone hating you, I know that's not true. Possibly you've gotten off on the wrong foot with a few people, but I don't think all is lost. You're a strong and determined person, Kelly. If you apply those traits to improving your behavior, I'm sure you'll feel happier here."

Andrea stood up and stretched. "It's almost three. Let's get you back to your room. You must be exhausted. Tomorrow, we'll talk this all over with Dr. Wainwright. I don't know what the penalty will be for breaking curfew, but if you tell him what happened honestly, I'm sure he'll be fair and sympathetic."

It was strange climbing the broad staircase so late at night with no danger of being caught. Kelly quietly took off her heels in the hall, her habit since the night she'd woken up her suite mates, and undressed in the common room so as not to disturb Sheela. The space between her collarbones, where the locket normally sat, felt bare and strange. Kelly slipped into bed and lay in the dark, reliving the day's events and wondering what the morning would bring. Whatever punishment she received, it couldn't be any worse than what she had already been through.

Kelly slept until close to noon. She woke up feeling nauseous and headachy, but strangely ravenous. After a long, tepid bath, she dragged herself down to the cafeteria, where she talked Signora Peretti into making her some

pastina en brodo, Italian chicken noodle soup. She ate quickly, wanting desperately to get out of there before Joe showed up. She had no idea how she'd react when their paths crossed.

Why on earth hadn't she told Andrea the truth? She owed Joe and Rodney absolutely nothing, and yet she had protected them. Old habits die hard, she supposed; admitting to mistakes was never one of Kelly's great strengths. She ran over the list of conditions her father had drafted before she came to Italy. She had signed her name on the dotted line, gone to Italy, and blown several of them in just over a month. Even by her own rather creative standards, Kelly was failing miserably.

Joe had turned out to be such a disappointment. And yet they'd had so much fun together. Their first kiss, sunny afternoons spent exploring the city, evenings in the lounge playing video games or listening to music. She remembered the way it felt all the times Joe held her close as they danced into the small hours.

"I'm going to show you the best time you've ever had when you visit me in Cali," Joe had promised. "I swear; you've never been anywhere more beautiful. We'll spend every day on the beach, party with my friends every night. Watching the sun set over the ocean from my dad's deck in Malibu is the third-best thing in the world." She could almost feel his stubbly chin nuzzling her cheek as he leaned in and whispered in her ear. "Surfing and you are first and second."

What a load of crap. It was time for Kelly to face what she had been denying for weeks: that Joe needed to get drunk or high almost every day. That he lied as easily as he breathed. And worst of all, that he didn't really care about her—he just wanted a partner in crime. Oh God. Wasn't that exactly what she had wanted, too?

Andrea appeared as Kelly was finishing her soup and looked her over in her usual thoughtful, appraising way. "How are you feeling today?"

"Okay, thanks. A little tired, I guess." She forced a smile, but the corners of her mouth quivered. Ditching her bowl, she followed Andrea to the main level and down the hall to Dr. Wainwright's office.

The office looked exactly the way a professor's should: dark wood paneling, overstuffed floor-to-ceiling book-shelves, and exotic-looking artifacts piled on every sur-face. Kelly perched on the worn leather couch facing the vast desk, waiting for the interrogation that was sure to end her summer in Italy.

Her heart began to hammer as Dr. Wainwright ambled in, a large roll of paper tucked under his arm. She knew that whatever happened, he would be merciful; it was the thought that she'd disappointed him and Andrea that

bothered her the most. And she couldn't even imagine her parents' reaction. She'd be sent home in disgrace, grounded for at least the first semester of senior year; they'd probably make her skip the prom, too. Whatever any of the adults decided, Kelly couldn't say she'd blame them: She had botched this big-time.

The mantel clock above the fireplace ticked like a time bomb in the still room. Kelly tore at a cuticle and watched a tiny bead of blood appear and slowly spread until finally she stuck her finger in her mouth. One thing was for sure: Dr. Wainwright was in no rush to end her misery. He carefully fished his reading glasses from his shirt pocket, put them on, and began reading from a folder, page after page. The mysterious roll of paper rested on the desk beside him. At long last, he glanced up at her.

"So, Andrea tells me that she discovered you on her doorstep early this morning, quite a while after curfew. Is that true?"

"Yes, sir." Kelly couldn't meet his warm eyes.

"Can you tell me what happened?"

"It's just like I told Andrea, sir. I went out with some friends—way before curfew—and we danced for a while. Then an emergency came up and my friends had to leave. They told me to wait for them, which I did until I realized how late it was. Then I called a cab and came straight back here."

"That's not exactly what you told me, Kelly." Kelly had

almost forgotten that Andrea was in the room, she had been so still and silent. "You said you lost your friends, but you never mentioned an emergency. That sounds serious."

Kelly cursed herself for not keeping the details of her story straight. Always state the facts truthfully. "This girl got sick and kind of passed out, and they had to take her home. She was Italian, not somebody from the program."

"You must have been frightened." Dr. Wainwright's voice remained friendly and calm. This was not the bawling out she expected at all.

"I was, I guess. I was pretty angry at my friends, but later on I got worried. I still don't know if they got home or not." Actually, she was furious, and she wasn't at all sure she cared whether Joe and Rodney were back in one piece.

Dr. Wainwright pressed his fingertips together and rested his chin on them. "Kelly, every day of our lives, we each create a self-portrait. As we define ourselves, we erase a bit here, add a bit there, make this side more colorful or that one more subdued. Each experience adds more depth to the picture." He grinned. "I'm still a work in progress, obviously." Kelly nodded and tried to smile back. She hadn't a clue what this philosophical rambling could possibly have to do with her being expelled from the program.

"I suspect that at home, you're a very well-adjusted person. You have a certain stature in your school, in your community, and in your family. Here, you were asked to start with a blank slate, to adjust all over again."

"I haven't adjusted at all," Kelly blurted.

Dr. Wainwright smiled. "When I first moved here, I felt like I was on Mars. It took me time to appreciate the many charms of Italy and its people, and even more time for them to appreciate me. Now I wouldn't trade living in Rome for anywhere else in the world.

"But we're here to talk about you, and how we can make you feel more at home here." He began unfurling the roll of papers that he'd brought in with him, revealing several of Kelly's drawings. "This morning Andrea showed me some of the work you've done in her studio-arts class."

Andrea's class was Kelly's favorite. The drawing and painting were pretty fun, and she was crazy about Andrea. She had genuinely been interested when the stone carver visited class to talk about his work restoring churches, and when the fresco painter taught them to make tempera paint the old-fashioned way, using egg yolks and bright, powdered pigments. Those two hours were always the fastest-moving part of Kelly's day.

Dr. Wainwright was still flipping through the pages of her artwork, squinting rather comically and turning them every which way. She hoped her drawings didn't reveal that she was crazy or anything.

"I'm not the expert Andrea is, but I think these drawings are absolutely marvelous. You have a wonderful, free style and a color sense that really reflects your exuberant personality. I think you're a very talented young woman." He looked at her over the top of his glasses, smiling.

For once, Kelly was speechless. Now that he mentioned it, she had always gotten pretty decent grades in art. And Andrea always went out of her way to compliment Kelly in class. But she had never expected to receive such strong praise from Dr. Wainwright, especially today.

"What I'm worried about, Kelly, is that you're not making very good use of your free time here, and both the PIR and the S.A.S.S. program have high standards to uphold." Dr. Wainwright removed his glasses and leaned across the desk toward her. "May I be completely open with you?"

Brace yourself for impact. "Sure, I guess so."

"I'm sorry to say this, but I think that Joe Leahy is the worst person you could ally yourself with right now. His behavior has become increasingly erratic and irresponsible since he's been here. I strongly suspect that he is the catalyst for your lateness and lack of preparation in class on several occasions. And I'll wager he was one of the friends you were out with last night."

Kelly bit her lip. Dr. Wainwright knew far more than she had thought about her many missteps this summer. She wondered if Sheela had ratted her out. Dr. Wainwright was clearly waiting for her to speak, but she couldn't think of a thing to say.

"I had no choice but to notify your parents about your recent tardiness to your classes and your violation of curfew last night," Dr. Wainwright said. "We want you to stay

in the program, Kelly, but it's school policy to keep parents informed about this type of behavior. They're as concerned about you as we are."

A droplet of sweat crawled down Kelly's back. So her parents knew. Kelly had thought she'd just have to explain what happened to the locket; now her upcoming conversation with them was going to be even more painful.

Dr. Wainwright handed the sketches back to Andrea. "Andrea is putting together a small group of gifted students to paint a mural on the south wall of the dining room. It will involve a lot of hard work, and will probably take up much of your free time.

"We've been thinking that a composite of some of Rome's most cherished sites would create a beautiful vista. The decor down there, as you know, leaves something to be desired." Dr. Wainwright gazed at Kelly with his lively blue eyes. "What do you say?"

"It sounds great. What's the catch?"

Dr. Wainwright threw back his head and guffawed. Even Andrea's mouth twitched slightly.

"Besides your promise to be absolutely punctual to class from now on, there's only one real catch. I must ask you to reduce your time with Joe to a minimum. Before the two of you get into real trouble, this friendship needs to go on the back burner. Otherwise, I'm fairly certain that one of you will end up heading home early."

Kelly nodded slowly. "I understand. And I think you're right about me and Joe. I'll take care of it."

Dr. Wainwright smiled sadly. "I know it won't be easy, but it truly is for the best."

"I'm sure you're right." Kelly nodded. "And I think I'll enjoy working on the mural."

"I know you'll be a wonderful asset to the team," Dr. Wainwright said. Andrea nodded and smiled in agreement.

Kelly stood up to go. "Thank you for having faith in me."

She trudged up the four flights to her room, utterly drained. Kelly had envisioned so many ways this meeting would end, and none of them involved her staying. Maybe she really did deserve to be here; the compliments Dr. W and Andrea gave her had certainly seemed sincere. It was time to end the pity party and drag a few small victories out of the smoking wreckage of her summer.

Joe appeared at Kelly's bedroom door only minutes after she finished with Dr. W and immediately grabbed her up in a crushing bear hug. "I've been out of my mind worrying about you, babe. Where have you been? I've come up here six times already."

Sheela, who was sitting at her desk in the common room, rolled her eyes. She pointedly turned her back on them and returned to her reading assignment. Kelly shut the bedroom door. She had no idea what she was going to

say, but she certainly didn't want Sheela to hear it.

"I just got totally reamed by Dr. W and Andrea. I had to wake her up last night to get into the building, and they're both megapissed at me. They even called my parents."

Kelly was exaggerating; as far as she was concerned, Dr. W and Andrea had been incredibly fair with her. But she wanted to make Joe feel as guilty as possible. He deserved it after what he had put her through. "Now I have to work on some special mural project. Where the hell were you guys? You were supposed to come back for me, remember?"

Joe's face was the picture of remorse. *Aargh.* The last thing she wanted was for him to be sweet right now. "It was pretty bad, Kel. Laura puked for like an hour straight, and when we brought her home, her father basically threatened to kill me and Rod. We were all the way over by Trastevere, and we couldn't get a cab. We didn't get back till like four A.M." He sat on the bed and looked up at her winningly. "How could you think I'd forget about you?"

Kelly felt herself wavering, but shook it off. "Look, I covered your asses this time, but I'm not gonna do it again. I don't even understand why I did it—anyone with half a brain would have hung you out to dry after what you did to me, not to mention poor Laura. You drugged us, for God's sake! I don't think I can trust you anymore."

Joe was hanging his head, but his face still wore its usual smirk. "Seriously, Kel, I think you're making a big deal out of nothing, don't you? I just wanted to make you feel better."

"How dare you say that! I was terrified, stuck at that club all by myself. And now Dr. Wainwright is making me work on some art project so he can keep an eye on me." She paused, cheeks flaming. "He specifically said you and I shouldn't hang out anymore."

To her surprise, Joe smiled broadly. "But that's so cool, like Romeo and Juliet. Sneaking around is a great way to spice up a relationship." He leaned in for a kiss, but Kelly pushed him away.

"What the hell is wrong with you? Have you heard one word I said? Keep it up, Joe—you'll end up getting expelled. We're definitely finished."

Joe stared at her for a long moment, his eyes blazing with anger. Then his mouth twisted into a sarcastic smile. "Whatever, Kel." He threw open the door and strode out of the room.

Kelly slammed the bedroom door and fell back on her bed, sobbing. Her summer was completely ruined. In one lousy week, she had lost her locket, her boyfriend, and her oldest friend.

She lay there for what seemed like hours. Finally, Sheela came in and sat down next to her. "I couldn't help overhearing your conversation with Joe. That took serious guts, you know."

"You think so?" Kelly felt a small glimmer of hope. Maybe it was still possible to make things right with Sheela.

Sheela nodded. "Joe can be as charming and persuasive as you—just in a creepy, weaselly way." She handed Kelly a tissue. "If you didn't have so much backbone, you easily might have caved. I'm proud of you."

If Kelly hadn't been so miserable, she would have smiled. "That means a lot to me. Especially after—you know, everything. I'm really sorry I've been a jerk."

Sheela nodded and stood up. "Listen, Jarvis and I are going to the Borghese Gardens. Do you want to come? The view of the city at sunset is supposed to be really gorgeous."

"And romantic," Kelly added. "I don't think you need me tagging along on your date. It is a date, isn't it?" Sheela didn't answer, but her cheeks flushed purple.

"Anyway, I have to tell my parents I lost the locket. And Dr. W called them about my being late to class and stuff. They're going to be furious at me. Might as well bite the bullet and get it over with." Kelly wiped her eyes and reached for her cell phone.

Sheela thought that ending things with Joe took back-bone? Once Kelly realized what kind of person he was, it had almost been easy. This phone call, on the other hand, was going to be pure agony. She couldn't make up for all the things she had done, but facing them was a good first step.

Her father picked up on the first ring.

"Hi, Dad," Kelly said, trying to keep her voice from shaking.

"Kelly, I was just thinking about you. Mom and I were planning to call you later today."

Kelly winced. Her dad was using his courtroom voice— a voice not to be reckoned with.

"I heard from Dr. Wainwright earlier this morning," he continued. "I wasn't happy to hear that you broke curfew. And he says you've been late to class repeatedly. Is that true?"

"Yes, Dad," Kelly whispered. "I'm really sorry."

"You should be. You promised us you'd keep up your grades and make a real effort this summer. This is especially embarrassing for us since Dr. Wainwright is a friend of Sheela's father."

"I know," Kelly said quietly, her eyes filling with tears. "I'm going to try harder. I promise." She took a deep breath. "Is Mom around? I need to talk to her about something else."

Kelly's heart was hammering so hard she could almost hear it.

"She's working the overnight shift at the ER to cover for another one of the nurses. She's not home yet."

"Oh." She'd just have to tell him and get it over with. "Actually, Dad," the words rushed out, "it's Grandma's locket. I was out with a friend the other night, and it must have slipped off my neck. I don't know how. Mom's gonna hate me." Kelly's voice quavered.

There was silence on the other end of the phone. "Dad?"

"I'm here, hon." Kelly heard him sigh. "Your mom will love you no matter what, but she is going to be upset. I'll talk to her when she gets home."

Kelly felt a rush of guilt. If she hadn't been so intent on partying with Joe, she might have noticed when the locket fell off.

"I know how much it meant to Mom. I can't believe how badly I've messed up everything." She sniffled.

Her father sighed again. "Listen, everyone deserves an appeal now and then, so consider this your get-out-of-jail free card. I'll let this slide for now. But I don't want to get another call from Dr. Wainwright, unless it's to tell us how great you're doing. Understand?"

"Completely," Kelly said, nodding into the phone.

"Honey? I've got a brief to write this morning for a new case. Can we talk again later?"

"Sure," Kelly said, relieved that the conversation was almost over. "And Dad? Tell Mom I'm really sorry."

"I'll make sure to."

Kelly shut off her phone, wondering what else she'd have to apologize for before this summer was over.

Chapter Nine

To: kelcat@email.com

From: m&ebrandt@email.com

Subject: Your grandmother's locket

Dear Kelly,

Dad told me what happened with Grandma's locket. I can't pretend that I'm not heartbroken that it's lost, and I'm certainly not happy that you were breaking curfew when you lost it. Maybe, if we're lucky, it will still turn up.

I'll call you tomorrow so we can talk more. Please don't

forget the promise you made us about sticking to your studies. Dad and I know how hard you worked to get into the program, and we'd hate to see you lose out on the great opportunities there. We just want you to do well.

Love,
Mom

Kelly smiled as Andrea loaded her six mural painters onto the metro for a trip to an art-supply shop near the Pantheon. She was excited not to be spending the afternoon cooped up at school. Having her free time so strictly regimented was actually a big relief. At home, her weekend plans were usually squared away by Tuesday afternoon, dinnertime at the latest. Only a week after her split with Joe, Kelly was already feeling the same odd desperation—loneliness, mere mortals called it—creeping up on her again, as it had when she first arrived in Rome.

As they rode the train, Kelly checked out the other members of the group. The male–female ratio totally sucked—five to one—and the lone guy was Dai, an intense Japanese kid from Kelly's Italian class. He was absorbed in sketching a wildly detailed, sci-fi creature of some sort on the back of his notebook. Gabriela, whose sneakers were spattered with paint, was obviously a serious artist—Kelly had seen her stuff hanging up in the art studio. Hildy and Veronica, whom Kelly had never seen talking to anyone except each other, were deep in a heated discussion about the "lines of incongruity" evident in Botticelli's works. Compared to them, Sheela was a party animal. Kelly was almost relieved to see Goth Girl, otherwise known as Marina, finishing off the group. At least Kelly had spoken to her before, even if the conversation had failed miserably.

Andrea laid out her plans for putting together the mural. "This week, we'll travel around the city, choosing landmarks to include in the piece. Then you'll each make preliminary pencil sketches. When those designs are finalized, you'll ink over the lines, copy them onto film, and project the images on the wall. When that's all done, we'll be ready to paint."

The group followed Andrea several blocks to a pretty little art store hidden away on a cobblestoned alleyway. Outside the door, an easel held an oil painting of the street they were standing on. The art shop was the central focus of the painting.

Kelly leaned over it, admiring the artist's deft brushstrokes and the way hues were subtly mixed to perfectly capture the warmth of the stones and the brightness of the red geraniums that sat outside the door. She didn't realize how absorbed she was until Andrea put a hand on her shoulder. "What do you think?"

"I wish I could paint like that," Kelly said. "I wonder who did it?"

Kelly thought she saw a hint of color rise in Andrea's cheeks. "Actually, I painted it. Whenever I'm in Rome, I stock up on art supplies here. Signor Carelli has always been so kind to me, I made this as a thank-you."

"It's amazing," Kelly said.

Andrea ushered them into the store, where an elderly man—presumably Signor Carelli—kissed Andrea noisily on both cheeks. He gave them the run of the store, and Andrea showed them all different kinds of materials: chalk sticks called Conte crayons, glass bottles filled with jewel-colored inks, and a variety of paints and pigments.

Hildy and Veronica ran over to a shelf of antique print books, while Dai browsed through some posters by a modern artist named Giorgio de Chirico. Marina had picked up a book on angels, and was studying each picture so closely her nose ring practically scraped the page. A Goth who was into angels? Go figure.

Kelly wandered around the store, picking up brushes and pens and examining the artwork on the walls. Everyone else in the group seemed to have a real passion for art; Kelly didn't even know if she had her own style. Maybe with this mural, she could really make something that was special, like Andrea's painting of the store.

Finally, armed with large pads and a handful of pencils and Conte crayons, the group continued on to the Pantheon, which Kelly hadn't seen yet. Andrea explained that the building combined a Greek-style temple with a

Roman dome. It was pretty amazing: a huge, impressive hunk of stone plopped right in the middle of a crowded piazza.

The Pantheon was the best-preserved ancient building Kelly had seen so far. Pieces of the original marble facade still clung to the two-thousand-year-old walls, and a row of elaborate pillars framed gargantuan bronze entrance doors. But the most striking part was the vast, domed roof. Andrea said it was one of the greatest feats of engineering in the world. The builders had built it on a huge, round hill of dirt, and then took the earth away when construction was completed.

Inside, the dome was equally impressive—when Kelly looked up at it, a ray of sunlight beamed all the way down to her feet.

"The hole in the center of the roof is called the oculus," Andrea told them. "It provides all the light in here, and as the sun travels west through the sky, the sunshine moves around the room.

"As an art historian, my favorite fact about the Pantheon is that the Renaissance painter Raphael is buried here." Andrea walked over to his alcove, which was watched over by two stern men who looked like older versions of Swiss Guards. A bunch of other big shots were also entombed in the building, a practice that was pretty common in Europe. Kelly found it utterly creepy.

After they had checked it out completely, the group sat

down at a café in the bustling square outside, ordered cappuccinos, and began sketching. "Remember," Andrea said, "I want you to feel free to draw in your own style. Whether that's anime, Abstract Expressionist, or Pointillist, so be it. Don't worry about stuff like proportion and perspective yet—this is a warm-up. We'll draw first and decide how to put it all together later." As they worked, she snapped photos of the building from different angles and occasionally peeked over their shoulders.

Marina leaned over toward Kelly. "What's your glitch, Katie? I didn't know Head Cheerleader Barbie was into mixing paint. Aren't you worried you'll ruin your pretty outfit?"

"Actually, it's Kelly." She was a little miffed that Marina still couldn't remember her name. "Dr. Wainwright thought I had too much time on my hands. I broke curfew a bunch of times to go clubbing and he found out about it. So here I am. As for my glitches, I have way too many to mention."

Marina looked impressed. "Killah Kelly. I think I underestimated you." She held up a hand. "What do you think? 'Eighty-one Pontiac Firebird, graphite gray.'"

Kelly tilted her head appraisingly. "It's okay, but wouldn't a nice Italian import, maybe an Alfa Romeo or a Ferrari, be more appropriate?"

The ice cracked, and Goth Girl giggled.

They roamed the city for the rest of the day, and Kelly discovered that Andrea seemed to know everything about

Rome. She walked the city like a native, navigating little alleys where Kelly would have become hopelessly lost and leading her group through the insane traffic with calmness and skill. On the way to their destinations, she would often stop to point out a building where some famous author or artist had lived, or a particularly beautiful detail on a church that they would never have noticed otherwise.

"How do you know all this?" Kelly asked her.

"When I was growing up, I spent a month here every summer, visiting family. Hanging out with my Roman cousins was always the high point of my year. When it was time to go home, I would cry for two days straight."

Kelly looked at Andrea's placid face and tried to picture it puffy-eyed and snot-streaked. Impossible.

Andrea read her skeptical expression. "You know, not everybody loves their high-school experience."

Marina snorted. "You can say that again. You know Dante's rings of hell? My high school makes up at least three of them. And it's in Arizona, so it's even hotter than hell."

Andrea laughed sympathetically. "I was miserable when I was a teenager. This was the one place where I felt I belonged."

Kelly rolled her eyes. "Please, look at you. I bet you had tons of boyfriends and were super popular."

Andrea raised an eyebrow. "Kelly, you wouldn't have given me the time of day when I was a teenager. I didn't

go out on one date in high school, and if someone had asked me out, I probably would have died of fright. I was completely socially clueless."

Hildy and Veronica, almost in unison, nodded understandingly. But Kelly's mind boggled at the thought of Andrea as a socially challenged outcast.

"Anyway, I'm living testimony that there is life after high school. Once I got to college, I found that people were a lot more accepting if you were a little bit different."

"I'm not holding my breath for that," Marina said.

Andrea waved the group across Via del Corso and down the street toward the Piazza di Spagna. "Enough of my life story. I want each of you to tell me who your favorite Italian artist is, and why. You first, Dai."

Kelly inwardly groaned. Just when things were starting to get interesting, Andrea always sent them back to the drawing board.

To: tyffaniandco@email.com

From: kelcat@email.com

Subject: When in Rome. . . buy leather!

Dear Tyff,

It was great hearing from you—can't wait to hear your voice and see your face soon. Wish you and Starr were here to go shopping with me—the stores in Rome are outrageous. Unfortunately, the exchange rate on the euro stinks, so the prices are pretty outrageous, too! Still, I want to buy a leather jacket, if I can do it without my vegan roommate noticing.

Next week we're going away for a while, to Siena and Florence. My Italian teacher (great legs—coaches the school soccer team) says that they speak the purest form of Italian there. Maybe I stand half a chance of understanding what people are saying, for once!

After that, we're going to Pompeii and Naples. It's supposed to be pretty interesting down there—tons of ancient ruins and whatnot. If you don't get any e-mails for a couple of weeks, you'll know why.

Love ya XXXX,
Kel

Once again, Kelly found herself standing in St. Peter's Square. This time, the mural group had come to take photos and work on sketches. They had visited each spot to make drawings except Kelly's. Andrea had mischievously requested that Kelly choose the Vatican as her landmark, and Kelly had to admit it was a little bit funny. Still, even though they weren't going into any of the buildings, Kelly made sure to wear her linen drawstring pants and a T-shirt instead of a tank.

As they walked toward the Basilica, Kelly gazed up at

the countless arches and columns, wondering at the intricacy of it all. How was she going to include all those details? There were like a hundred statues on top of the building alone.

Thinking of all the work she was taking on, Kelly asked Andrea the million-euro question. "We're gonna be gone two weeks on the field trip—how will we be able to finish the entire mural when we get back to Rome? We'll only have like three weeks left."

Andrea laughed. "I think we can do it. If we really run into trouble, we'll call in the Swiss Guard to help."

Kelly and Marina looked at each other and groaned. Dai was buried in one of his drawings, so it was tough to tell how he was taking it. Hildy and Veronica blinked anxiously.

"Six buildings in three weeks?" Gabriela cried.

"Hey, I'd rather work on this than conjugate verbs any day," Kelly said.

"Remember," Andrea told them. "The mural qualifies as your final project. That means that you have a jump on the rest of the students in the program, who won't even start their projects until we return from the field trip."

Kelly's eyes wandered over to the tourist information office. She had a sudden idea. "I'm gonna buy a few postcards—that way I can work on some drawings while we're away."

Kelly fluffed her hair, brushed on some lip gloss, and walked into the tourist information office. The postcards would come in handy, but she was also wondering whether Luigi, the sweet guy who had salvaged her first trip to the Vatican, would be around. It would be nice to hear his cute accent again. Sure enough, Luigi was behind the desk, speaking to a cluster of middle-aged tourists toting camcorders.

He was cuter than Kelly remembered—tall and thin, with close-cropped light brown hair and little wire-rimmed glasses that made him look smart but funky. She browsed through the postcards while she waited for the tourists to leave, then stepped up to the counter.

"Hi. Do you remember me?"

Luigi stared at her for a moment before smiling broadly. "I do! Did my note help you? Were you able to find your friends?"

"It did, and I did. I even got to see some of the galleries. I'm here working on a project and I needed to pick up some postcards, so I thought I'd come and say thanks again. You were a real lifesaver."

Luigi lowered his head modestly. "I'm so happy that it worked out well. And I'm even more happy that you came back to visit me."

"Me, too." Kelly smiled. "So, how long have you worked here?"

"For two summers. During the school year I study engineering at the university, La Sapienza. I'm hoping to work in the great tradition of Romans before me, who built the

Pantheon and the aqueducts—not to design another Tower of Pisa." He flashed the same grin she remembered from their first meeting.

A college boy and Roman, too—absolutely perfect!

"Maybe the pope will ask you to design a new wing here at the Vatican," Kelly teased. "Those galleries are pretty crowded."

Luigi threw back his head and laughed.

"Maybe we can meet up for a latte sometime," Kelly offered.

"That would be my great pleasure, signorina."

Kelly scribbled her cell number on the back of a gallery map. Luigi read it carefully. "Kelly Brandt. A very pretty name. *Piacere, Signorina Kelly.*"

"I'll be away for the next couple of weeks, but after that I hope you'll give me a call."

"*Certo.* I look forward to it very much."

Kelly paid for her postcards and virtually skipped out of the office, giving her hair a shampoo-commercial toss for good measure. The old Kelly was back, and better than ever.

Dr. Wainwright was sitting out the trip, keeping the program going for the full-time students. The night before they left, he gathered everyone in the lounge for a pep talk. "Over the last six weeks, I have watched each of you change and grow. I hope the next two weeks will be deeply enriching and moving for you. You'll come back here transformed by your visits to a veritable treasure trove of Italy's most special places."

Out of the corner of her eye, Kelly could see Joe snickering at Rodney. That jackass. After just a couple of weeks, she was having a hard time remembering what she had seen in Joe.

She switched her focus back to Dr. W's travelogue. "You'll start your journey in the delightful city of Siena—one of my favorite places on earth. I could spend a week in the cathedral alone. It's a big university town—something to think about when you're filling out those college applications." He chuckled. "Siena is surrounded by beautiful countryside. Try to stay awake on the train to soak in the scenery.

"When you leave Siena—reluctantly, I'll wager—you'll continue on to Firenze, or Florence, where your trusty guides will take you to the Duomo, the Ponte Vecchio, and the Uffizi Gallery, among other marvelous spots."

Dr. Wainwright's eyes widened dramatically. This was obviously his favorite part of the trip. "And then, you'll journey south"—he swept his arms downward—"to Naples and Pompeii. Those of you who are particularly interested in classical art and architecture will be in heaven. And the rest of you won't have anything to sneeze at, either.

"Besides being the birthplace of pizza, Napoli is home to the National Archaeological Museum. Most of the

artifacts excavated from Pompeii and Herculaneum are housed there. Seeing these items will help bring those cities to life for you as you walk among their ruins."

Kelly glanced over at Sheela, whose face was positively shining. Jarvis sat next to her, holding her hand. Sheela had been ridiculously happy since she'd hooked up with Jarvis.

Sheela smiled over at Kelly. "I've been dying to see Pompeii since I was a kid. I've read that once you see it, you never forget it."

Kelly feared that all this archaeology on top of the Pompeii trip could cause Sheela to have some sort of seizure. She had never seen her friend this enthusiastic about anything, not even when the Westlake marching band got on the evening news.

Dr. Wainwright was winding up his monologue. He smiled expansively and spread his arms wide. "With that, I beseech you to go forth, explore, and enjoy. I can't wait to hear all about your adventures in a fortnight."

Some of the students headed upstairs to pack. With all the art stuff going on, Kelly hadn't even figured out what clothes she wanted to bring.

Sheela's bag, of course, was already packed, *and* she had laid out her clothes for the next day. She and Jarvis were sitting on the couch together when Kelly walked in.

"Hey, Sheela," Kelly said, "would you mind if I roomed

with Marina on the field trip? I already asked her and she's cool with it."

Sheela looked up at her, frowning.

"Don't you think you should have asked me first?" she huffed. "Now I have to find a new roommate."

Kelly sighed. She had thought she was finally learning to be a better friend, and now she'd botched things with Sheela again. "I'm really sorry. I just figured you'd welcome a break from me."

"Well, I will now." Jarvis gave Sheela's shoulder a squeeze, and Kelly was relieved to see her face soften a bit. "Two weeks without listening to you snore or watching you coordinate outfits every morning? Maybe switching roommates isn't such a bad idea, after all." Sheela smiled. "Tell Marina I wish her the best of luck."

Chapter Ten

They left for Siena at the crack of dawn, silently dragging their bags out of the metro and through Stazione Termini. "Everybody keep a close eye on your stuff," Steve told them. "There are plenty of people hanging out here who would like to take it home."

Kelly was tired and cranky; she had been digging through her storage cage until 1 A.M., assembling her trip wardrobe. She couldn't wait to settle into her seat, crack open the latest issue of *Lucky,* and get this show on the road.

There was a mild traffic jam on the platform as the kids jostled to board the crowded train. Sheela and Jarvis had already disappeared into a mass of people inside. Kelly and Marina finally squeezed through the door and found a couple of seats together.

The train was loaded with commuters, all shouting into cell phones. Even though the group was in a nonsmoking car, cigarette stink drifted in from other cars, making Kelly's eyes itch and her nose run. Rain was falling on the farmland outside the streaky window, and Dr. W's spectacular views were shrouded in mist.

Kelly sighed. "This train's like a cattle car. How do people do this every day?"

Next to her, Marina cackled. "Don't tell me the queen of perky is out of sorts? Listen; it's a hundred and twelve degrees back in Tucson right now. My dad and brothers are all stuffed under the hood of some car or other, and there are two months' worth of dirty dishes waiting for me in the kitchen sink. I'm loving it here." She settled back and opened her sketchbook.

"How many brothers do you have?" Kelly asked.

"Three," Marina said. "I'm the youngest. Hurry up—you're allowed two more questions before I reach saturation."

Kelly grinned. Slowly but surely, Marina was opening up.

"What kind of cars do they fix?"

"Classics, mainly. Hot rods, too." Marina held up an electric-blue fingernail. "This is from a '65 Mustang convertible they're working on right now."

"Does your mom work at the garage, too?"

Marina's face tightened and she hunched over her sketch pad. "Sorry, Brandt. Interrogation's over."

Kelly sighed and opened her magazine. Marina was a tough nut to crack, but Kelly vowed to keep chipping away until she got through to her.

A few hours later the train pulled into Siena. The rain was really coming down, and they ran beneath an over-hang outside the station, waiting for a bus to take them into the center of town. Kelly had spent the last fifteen minutes on the train doing her makeup, but now it was sluicing down her face.

Finally, a little bus lurched to the outside curb and car-ried them up a steep hill to the center of the city. Siena was a labyrinth of narrow, winding streets, clearly not designed for traffic heavier than horses and carts. The bus driver soon pulled up beside a larger, busier piazza and, after a rapid conversation with Andrea, took off for the hotel with their luggage.

Marina watched him go, wearing her usual smirk. "I hope we're going to see those bags again. I'm soaked clean through to my undies, and I'm not gonna be happy if I have to wear this outfit for the next two weeks."

Kelly looked at her. Black pleated kilt with a skull pin holding it shut, black fishnet tank with a snake-print tube top underneath, ripped fishnet stockings, and combat boots. As far as she could tell, all of Marina's getups were exactly the same.

"Tell you what," Kelly replied. "If they lose our stuff, we'll go shopping and pick out whole new wardrobes."

Marina checked out Kelly's flirty, vintage ensemble, which was now sopping wet and drooping. "Yeah, I'm sure we'll find a one-stop emporium that will suit both of our sartorial needs."

They reached a large piazza, shaped like half an oval and ringed by little cafés and souvenir shops. "This is the Piazza del Campo, the heart of Siena," Steve explained. "Over there is the Palazzo Pubblico—town hall, and the Torre del Mangia, which, tragically, has nothing to do with eating." He rubbed his round belly. "The Palio, a crazy, competitive free-for-all on horseback, takes place in this piazza twice every summer, the way it has for centuries. If it ever stops raining today, we'll climb up to the top of the tower and take in an amazing view of Tuscany."

Steve waved them on toward one of the little streets leading out of the piazza. "Let's check out Il Duomo first. It's a great intro to Siena, and we'll escape the rain for a while."

The Duomo turned out to be a gargantuan church, and it was about the wildest-looking building that Kelly had ever seen. Andrea described it as "a masterpiece of Gothic architecture." It reminded Kelly of a wedding cake: white, with detailed carvings covering every inch of the marble front. Little figures of people and animals stood on every ledge and roof peak. Behind her, Kelly could hear Lisa

telling someone, "See what people were able to achieve before television ate away at their brains?" It was such a relief not to be rooming with her for the next couple of weeks.

The rain was letting up, and a gorgeous rainbow arced above the striped bell tower of the cathedral. The students followed the line of tourists inside, where, almost in unison, they gasped. The black and white marble stripes were repeated on the walls and columns of the interior, leading up dozens of feet to a ceiling magnificently painted in blue and gold. On the floor, enormous stone mosaics depicted scenes from the Bible in breathtaking detail. "We're allowed to walk on this?" Kelly asked.

Andrea laughed. "People have been walking on these floors for hundreds of years, Kelly."

Andrea and Steve walked back and forth among the groups, pointing out an important stained-glass window or a particularly beautiful panel of inlaid wood. "I know there's a lot to absorb here, but don't forget to look at the sculptures. Whoever can show me a Bernini or a Michelangelo gets a gelato later," Andrea told them.

They emerged from the cathedral over an hour later to find that the day had turned hot and sunny. Steve surveyed the bright sky and glanced at his watch. "How about some lunch, guys?" Steve could always be counted on to make sure nobody missed a meal. They trekked back through a warren of sloping little streets to a bustling outdoor café back in the Piazza del Campo.

Kelly sat down next to Sheela at the long table and ordered a *té freddo*. Who knew that Italians loved iced tea so much? "Can you believe that place? I could have spent three more hours in there, at least."

Sheela looked up from her *insalata*, surprised. "Three hours? I didn't think you could concentrate on anything except shopping or boys for more than fifteen minutes."

"Well, nothing prepared me for how beautiful it was inside. The tour books didn't make a very big deal about it at all." She blushed slightly. "I bought the photo guide in the gift shop so I won't forget all the details."

Sheela smiled. "That's great. Maybe you'll loan it to me sometime." She turned to Jarvis, who was offering her a bite of his panino. "Yum, that's good. What's in it? Eggplant and ricotta?"

Kelly watched them talking, their smiling faces pressed close to each other, and felt like an intruder. They were so cute together—not mushy, not show-offy, just nice. Jarvis genuinely seemed to care about Sheela, and it was obvious she was crazy about him.

Kelly glanced down toward Joe, who was smirking at Minnie and saying something Kelly couldn't hear. Minnie was ignoring him, but her shoulders were hunched and her eyes blinked rapidly; Joe knew exactly how to get

under the poor girl's skin. When they were dating, Kelly had listened to Joe make fun of her roommates and never said a word in their defense. Now she felt her hackles rising. Minnie wasn't strong enough to laugh off his abuse, and Joe wouldn't stop until he got her to cry.

Casually, Kelly walked the length of the table and touched Minnie's shoulder like they were best friends. "There's an empty seat on our end. Come sit with us." Stunned, Minnie nodded, and fixing Joe with a look of pure hatred, followed Kelly to safety.

"Your ex-boyfriend is such an asshole," she hissed, her voice shaking. Kelly was surprised; she didn't know Minnie ever used that kind of language.

"I know. Sorry."

"Well." Minnie sniffed. "I'm just glad you dumped his rear end."

As Kelly returned to her seat and her salad, Sheela nodded and smiled at her.

Kelly grinned back and looked across the cobblestoned piazza at the graceful curve of red brick buildings that surrounded them. She really liked this little place—it was so different from anywhere she had ever been. And Siena seemed to be bringing out the best in her. Standing up for Minnie had made her feel great, much better than sticking it to Joe would have been on its own.

Kelly had been interested in style for her entire life. Now, even though it went against all of her natural instincts, she knew it was time for her to start concentrating a whole lot more on substance.

Dr. Wainwright was absolutely right—two days in Siena wasn't enough; it was a place straight out of a fairy tale. After six weeks in a big, noisy metropolis, Kelly found Siena safe, small, and easy to navigate. Getting lost wasn't even an option: There were street signs everywhere pointing out all the tourist attractions, and almost every street eventually led to the Piazza del Campo. Best of all, Siena was a city designed for walkers; its narrow streets and twisting alleyways couldn't handle heavy traffic, so Kelly had been able to explore without her usual worries of getting squashed.

She walked until her feet were burning. Andrea had given everyone a crash course in Gothic architecture, and one of their assignments was to identify as many examples of flying buttresses, mullions, parapets, and vaulted ceilings as they could. It was ridiculously easy; you couldn't turn a corner without discovering a tiny stone gargoyle or a gracefully arched window. But Kelly had kept exploring, long after she'd gotten bored with the assignment. Wandering the winding medieval streets with a bag of lemon cookies in one hand and her worksheets in the other, she felt like she had stepped back in time hundreds of years. She found herself slipping into a fantasy involving a medieval princess who looked a lot like herself and

a young nobleman who bore an astonishing resemblance to Brad Pitt.

Now she was back on a bus heading for Florence, watching her little kingdom grow even tinier out the window. Outside the city, they passed by field after field of tidy rows of grapevines, which, according to Steve, would be made into Tuscany's famous wines. Green farmland, dotted with enormous rolled cylinders of hay and grazing animals, stretched for miles.

She glanced over at Marina, in the seat next to her. She had her head down, and her pencil scratched across the pages of her sketchbook with even more urgency than usual. Kelly tried peeking over the edge. "Can I see?"

Marina hugged the pad tightly to her chest. "Back off, Brandt!" She grinned, seeing Kelly's stung expression. "Relax. I'll show you when I'm good and ready. Might even ask you for a little help on it."

Kelly turned back to the window. She wasn't going to get any information from Marina right now; they were already following the huge painted "Firenze" sign painted on the highway lanes. The faint outline of the city loomed in the distance. As far as Kelly could tell from the outskirts, Florence was a big, modern city—not the Renaissance wonderland Dr. W had described.

As they pulled off the *autostrada,* Steve pointed out the window at the river running alongside the road. "This is the Arno, which divides Florence into two halves. We'll be spending a lot of time on this side of the river, in the Centro Storico. But the other side of the river has two spots we can't miss—the Pitti Palace and the Boboli Gardens."

Eventually, the bus pulled in front of a modest-looking little hotel. The kids gathered in the threadbare lobby while Andrea checked everybody in. Marina looked around dubiously, refusing to put her backpack down on the rug. "Kind of a dump, huh?"

"Who cares?" Kelly answered. "They have AC! At this point, I'd sleep in a litter box if it had air-conditioning." Their pensione in Siena had been cute, but it had been hot as hell.

Andrea held up her hands for silence. "Listen, everybody, this city is completely crammed with tourists this time of year. We've booked everything in advance, so it's essential that you get down here on time every morning." Kelly felt several kids' eyes on her and willed her cheeks not to go red.

"Let's go freshen up and meet back down here in half an hour to check out some of the sights in the Centro Storico."

Kelly shouldered her bag and headed upstairs to unpack.

That night, after trekking through the Duomo and touring two Renaissance palazzos, Kelly could barely keep her

eyes open long enough to brush her teeth. She finished in the bathroom and crawled into bed.

"It's all yours, Marina," she said.

"Already?" Marina deadpanned. "I figured you'd be in there at least another hour. Don't beauty-queen rituals last all night?"

"They certainly can," Kelly acknowledged. "But tonight I need my beauty sleep even more."

Marina climbed off her bed, knocking her sketch pad on the floor. Kelly caught a brief glimpse of pages filled with drawings of angels in all different styles, each with a face that looked strangely familiar to her. Kelly had seen that same face in several old photos clipped inside the cover of Marina's pad. The photos showed a woman sitting on a motorcycle. She was small and a little stocky, with a wide, carefree smile and dark, laughing eyes.

"Is that your mom?" Kelly asked, grabbing another quick look before Marina snatched the sketchbook.

"Was." Marina said. "She died last year."

Kelly's hand flew to her mouth. "Oh, I'm—"

"Don't say it! Do *not* say you're sorry. I can't stand the pity thing." Marina's look was threatening, "And don't think you're going to get me to spill the whole sob story."

"Okay," Kelly said quietly. "It's just that I remember you looking at that book of angel paintings the day we went to the art store for supplies."

"They're for my next tattoo. I want something special to

remember her by that I can carry with me all the time."

Kelly nodded. "I had something like that of my grandmother's. She died last year, too. It was a locket." Her hand moved up to her collarbone. "But I lost it."

"That's rough. At least I know once it's on me, the tat's not going anywhere." Marina headed for the bathroom, but abruptly stopped in the doorway.

"My mom had a rare heart defect, a total fluke. When she was in her thirties, she got a heart transplant, which worked great, until just over a year ago. The new heart gave out and she died before the doctors could find a new donor heart." Marina looked at the carpet, her voice tight. "I want to do something in her honor, you know? But it has to be absolutely perfect, 'cause she was perfect."

"It will be," Kelly said, just before Marina shut the bathroom door.

Chapter Eleven

"This woman needs a serious makeover," Kelly said, staring at the painting. A desperate, wide-eyed face, framed by a crown of slithery snakes, grimaced back at her from the wall.

Marina's eyes lit up. "Medusa—totally freakin' cool, man. That's what I'm talking about!"

Kelly and Marina were deep into their exploration of the Uffizi Gallery with the rest of the group on their second afternoon in Florence.

Looking at the mythical monster was supposed to turn you to stone, and Kelly could see why. "No wonder you like it—that's exactly what you looked like when you woke up this morning. Who's the artist?"

"My perfect man, Caravaggio. Did you know that he got thrown out of Rome for killing a guy during a tennis match? How's that for a temper? He lived fast, died young, and totally rocked the art world. Just my luck; he died four hundred years ago." Marina held her arms straight out, looking for an empty patch of skin. "Would this make a killer tattoo, or what?"

Kelly shrugged. "I thought your next tattoo was gonna be for your mom."

"That's my *next* tattoo—it's not gonna be my last." Marina grinned. "You can never have too many."

Kelly grabbed Marina's elbow and steered her away from Medusa. "Let's go check out the Botticelli room—he knew how to paint *beautiful* faces. I want to see *The Birth of Venus*—at least she won't give me nightmares."

Marina snorted. "This from the girl who looked upon the face of Joe Leahy and survived. Fine, let's go look at the pretty pictures, you big wuss."

As the group made their way from the Uffizi to the Accademia del' Arte, Kelly found herself feeling claustrophobic in the tourist-choked streets. Australians, Germans, Brits, and Americans were everywhere, lining up to see the Duomo, filling the piazzas, and milling around the leather stalls at the Mercato di San Lorenzo.

The more American tourists Kelly saw, the more embarrassed she felt. They were often slow, they were usually rude, and they automatically expected everyone to speak English. She realized that she probably looked just the same way to the locals. Kelly decided, right in the middle of Piazza San Lorenzo, that she was going to work much harder on her Italian. The next time she came to Italy, she at least wanted to be able to carry on a polite conversation. *The next time she came to Italy?* How had that thought popped into her head? Somehow, despite all the mistakes she'd made here, Italy had begun to grow on her.

The group slowly made its way into the Accademia del' Arte to see Michelangelo's *David*.

"The statue was recently cleaned—call it his five-hundredth birthday present," Andrea explained. "You're getting to see him in better shape than he's been in hundreds of years. In this sculpture, Michelangelo portrayed muscles and bones far more accurately than any other artist of his time."

Kelly walked around the statue, admiring the details Michelangelo had managed to coax from solid marble. She could even see the tiny veins in David's hands. She opened up her sketch pad and flipped back to the drawing she'd made in Andrea's class weeks ago. She compared it to the sculpture. Her version was okay, but it was nothing in comparison to the real deal.

Kelly felt a rough tap on her shoulder, and turned to see

Marina standing next to her, with her hands on her hips.

"As usual, everyone is waiting for you. I've been sent to pry you out of here."

"Sorry. He's just so amazing," Kelly said.

"You know, under your prom-queen exterior, you're actually a massive nerd." Marina smirked. "Unless you just dig ogling naked marble guys."

Kelly laughed. "I'll go with massive nerd. And coming from you, I'll take it as a compliment."

Kelly's favorite afternoon in Florence was spent wandering the grounds of the Boboli Gardens, the beautiful public park across the river. The view of the city was gorgeous from there, and although there were plenty of tourists around, the mood was serene and relaxed. Kelly and Marina trailed along after Sheela and Jarvis—he had been to Florence a bunch of times and knew a lot about the park's history.

"Look at this crazy statue!" Marina called out, pointing to a dwarf riding a turtle.

"A lot of the art here has a sense of humor," Jarvis said as Sheela beamed proudly at him. "It was an artistic style called Mannerism. The gardens were designed to entertain people who walked here."

Kelly was really enjoying spending time with Sheela again, and she wanted to do everything she could to make it last. And the more time she spent with Jarvis, the more

Kelly liked him. Unlike a lot of the kids in the program, he didn't treat Marina like a freak, and he didn't judge Kelly for her previous mistakes. She could see why Sheela was crazy about him.

"So this was the Renaissance version of an amusement park?" Kelly asked.

"You could say that. There used to be jets of water all over the place that would squirt up randomly and soak people. I'm not sure how funny they found it."

"If they were half as concerned about their hair as Kelly is, I'm guessing they hated it," Sheela deadpanned.

"Please, Sheela told me those Medicis had zillions of servants around to fix their hair," Kelly groused. "I, on the other hand, have to brave this humidity with a zero-watt blow-dryer and a pathetic travel-size bottle of Bed Head."

"And why are we so concerned about our hair, Kelly?" Sheela's smile widened. "Still expecting Orlando Bloom to materialize?"

Kelly blushed as an image of Luigi popped into her head.

Marina's eyes narrowed. "I swear, if you're thinking about Joe, Sheela and I are gonna hang you from the Ponte Vecchio by your perfect pink toenails."

Kelly felt strangely shy. "I was thinking about someone else, and believe me, he's the anti-Joe. Sheela, do you remember the guy I told you about, from the Vatican info center?"

She filled them in on her second encounter with Luigi, word for word.

"Has he called yet?" Marina demanded.

"No," Kelly said. "But I told him we'd be away for a while." She smiled. "Even if he doesn't, I can always use another bad wardrobe choice as an excuse to see him again."

After the gardens, they walked across the Ponte Vecchio, the ancient bridge that connected the two halves of Florence. Kelly had never seen a bridge with stores on it before—there were jewelry shops running its entire length. Gold shimmered in every window, and the kids ambled along, window-shopping. In the center of the bridge, Kelly stopped and leaned against the rail, watching the sun set over the Arno.

She didn't know Joe was behind her until his chin was resting on her shoulder. "Pretty, huh?"

Kelly straightened up, shaking him off. "Yeah, it's gorgeous."

"Romantic, right?" Joe gripped her hands and squeezed, looking deep into her eyes. "Listen, I really miss you."

Kelly glanced over her shoulder. Sheela and Marina were both watching, concern written all over their faces. Somehow, knowing they were there made her feel stronger. "I've been in so much trouble already, Joe. I can't risk screwing up again this summer. I'm sorry."

He didn't move. He kept gazing at her, an anguished look on his face. "You sure?" There was more than a hint of threat in those two words.

Kelly looked away. "Yup. I'm really sorry, Joe."

He dropped her hands and smiled. "Your loss, Kel." Then he turned and walked into the shadows.

When Sheela and Marina appeared at her side, Kelly realized she was shaking. "What the hell was that about?" Marina demanded. Kelly could have hugged them both, but PDAs were neither girl's style.

"It's okay. I think he finally got the message that it's over." The three of them leaned their elbows on the railing and watched the water gently lapping the ancient stones below them. Finally, Kelly felt she could relax.

Chapter Twelve

Their last morning in Florence, Marina and Sheela sat with Kelly at breakfast. Even though she suspected they were just there to scare Joe off, she enjoyed every minute of it. Kelly listened, slack-jawed with amazement, as Sheela held her own in an animated discussion of punk rock and alternative music. It turned out that all those hours Sheela spent reading, she had their local college radio station playing in the background.

"What's up with Andrea?" Sheela gestured with her chin. This morning Andrea seemed exhausted and preoccupied. Before breakfast, the girls had passed by her in the

hall, having an urgent-sounding conversation on her cell phone. As soon as she spotted them, she had stopped talking, watching until they stepped into the dining room.

Kelly had been too excited to notice. After getting a taste of the Tuscan countryside, she was dying to get out of the city and kick back a little. The group was visiting two villages, San Gimignano and Montepulciano, during the day. Then they were spending the night in the middle of an olive grove, at a pensione run by a farmer and his wife.

It sounded so romantic and charming, Kelly wished she had someone special to share it with. Her thoughts turned to Luigi once again. There was an air of genuine kindness and sincerity about him that made her want to get to know him better. She really hoped he'd call when she got back to Rome.

A well-aimed elbow from Marina jolted Kelly back to earth. "Don't look now, but Princess Prada is headed directly for you, and she doesn't look happy."

"Kelly, can I have a moment?" Andrea asked, motioning her aside.

"We'll see you on the bus, Kel," Sheela said, shooting her a puzzled look.

"It's important that I speak to you later, Kelly," Andrea said to her once they were out of earshot. "See me right after dinner, okay? Don't blow this off."

Kelly was a little miffed. She had been as punctual as an

atomic clock these past few weeks. Andrea, of all people, should know how hard she was trying to mend her bad reputation. And what was so serious that Andrea needed to keep it from Kelly's friends? She grabbed her bag and headed for the bus, forcing any bad thoughts from her mind.

"What was that about?" Marina asked when Kelly dropped into the seat next to her.

"No clue," Kelly replied. "She just said we needed to talk later. I don't get it; I haven't screwed up once during this trip."

Marina opened her novel. "Not even once? I'm sure we can think of something."

Normally, Kelly would have smiled, but Andrea's somber face loomed in her mind. Whatever it was she wanted to discuss, it sounded serious.

"There she blows, San Gimignano! A lot of people say the skyline reminds them of New York City. What do you think?"

Oddly enough, Kelly saw exactly what Steve meant. Even though it was set on a hill overlooking rolling green farmland, the little town's cockeyed stone towers bore a strange resemblance to skyscrapers.

"In medieval times, the higher you built, the richer you were. In this town's heyday, there were more than seventy

tall towers standing. Now, only thirteen are left. But they'll give you a good idea of what a thriving medieval community looked like."

At Poggibonsi, the group transferred to a local bus into town. "There are no cars allowed within the city walls, so get ready to do some walking," Steve announced cheerfully.

"I can't wait to show you guys some of the natural wonders in this part of the country," he added. "Here in Tuscany, you can learn a lot about nature just by walking into a local *enoteca*, where they sell food and wine. For instance, San Gimignano is known for growing *zafferano*, or saffron, the costliest spice in the world. They also grow a special variety of grape that makes their famous white wine, Vernacchia."

Food, wine, and spices. Kelly could deal with that. They entered the city through an imposing archway set into thick stone walls and found themselves on a bustling main street. Kelly busied herself with checking out the pretty shops while other students dutifully pulled out their workbooks and started scribbling. They only had a few hours to spend here before heading on to Montepulciano, the largest town in the area.

Still, as they strolled the winding lanes of San Gimignano and Montepulciano, Kelly found her buoyant mood punctured by little pinpricks of worry. Andrea's tone had been urgent, and she had looked so worn and frazzled at breakfast. Was there a problem at home? Had something happened to her parents? Kelly swiftly dismissed this theory; Andrea would have told her straight up. What was so crucial that they absolutely had to talk, yet could wait until after dinner, hours from now?

The clear, sunny afternoon gave way to a balmy, pink-tinged dusk. As they boarded yet another bus to go to the olive grove, Pulcinella, the strange clownlike figure who topped the clock tower in Montepulciano, raised his mechanical arm and struck the hour. Not so long now until her meeting with Andrea—Kelly's stomach tightened in dread.

The pensione was a long, flat stone building set on a sprawling plot of land planted with olive trees. The main farmhouse and several outbuildings were just opposite the inn. Their hosts, Ivano and Teresa Severino, along with their four friendly dogs, greeted them at the door.

It was late, so dinner was put on the table quickly. Like many meals in Italy, the food was served family-style—on huge platters passed from person to person. There was antipasto of grilled vegetables and homemade pasta for the main course. Teresa Severino explained what each dish was as it was set on the table. The kind, graceful woman reminded Kelly of her grandmother. She reached up to touch her locket, then caught herself. She wondered if her grandparents had stayed at a wonderful place like this on their honeymoon.

Kelly hadn't expected to have much of an appetite, but before she knew it, her plate was empty. Even Lisa the Tree Hugger scarfed down her linguini, pecorino cheese and all.

Big bowls of locally grown grapes and figs were put out for dessert. Each guest was poured a little glass of *vin santo*, sweet dessert wine. Kelly sat back in her seat, stuffed. This was one of the best meals she'd ever eaten, but she also felt like a prisoner who had just finished his final dinner before facing the firing squad.

Finally, Andrea led her down a hallway to a quiet office and motioned for her to sit. Kelly wished she hadn't eaten so much; her stomach was churning like a washing machine.

Andrea sighed, a pained look on her face. "Kelly, last night Dr. Wainwright received an anonymous e-mail telling him to search your locker for drugs." Kelly relaxed; unless he was looking for Midol and prescription zit cream, she was totally in the clear.

Silently, Andrea handed her a fax from Dr. Wainwright.

To: twainwright@pir.edu

From: afriend@email.com

Subject: Kelly Brandt

Dear Dr. Wainwright,

I am a concerned friend of Kelly Brandt's. She has developed a real problem with drugs and alcohol this summer. I am pretty sure that she has been using her storage space in the basement to hide her stash of marijuana. Unless action is taken, I'm afraid she'll harm herself.

I don't want to get Kelly in trouble. I'm writing to you because I care deeply about her, and want her to get the help she so desperately needs. Thank you for listening.

A Friend

Kelly read the message twice, then went back and looked at the e-mail address, trying to get some clue to the sender's identity. It was sent from a freebie mailbox that anyone could set up.

"Well, this is obviously some kind of stupid gag. I mean, Dr. Wainwright knows it's ridiculous—just tell him to go check my stuff."

"He already did. His search turned up a bag of pot and some other things." Andrea leaned forward and looked her straight in the eye. "Kelly, I don't want to believe this, but it's pretty damning evidence. Not only could he expel you immediately, Dr. Wainwright could level criminal charges against you."

The floor seemed to buckle and quake under Kelly's feet.

"I think it's time that you told me everything, especially about the night you broke curfew." Andrea's face was stern.

Kelly couldn't stop herself—the words came pouring out. "I was with Joe and Rodney, at a club in Ostiense. I don't remember the name. I could show you exactly where it is, though. Rodney was with this girl named Laura, she was Italian. I think Joe said she lived in Trastevere.

"Anyway, the guys brought us drinks. I only drank a little before I started to feel weird—kind of numb and groggy. Joe said he had put something in them to make us relax. It made Laura really sick. They basically had to carry her out of there."

Kelly stared down at her shaking hands. "You pretty much know the rest."

"Has Joe gotten you involved in using drugs?"

"No! I swear, Andrea, I'm not into that stuff. Plus, I'm completely allergic to smoke. I can prove it. I'll even take a drug test if you want."

Andrea seemed lost in thought. "Do you remember if your locker was empty when you put your bags in?"

"I don't know. Signor Peretti did it for me."

"Did anyone else have access to your locker? Could you have left the key out somewhere?"

Kelly felt her blood pressure rising. "Joe could have easily taken my key and copied it. I know he had a front-door key—that's how we got in the building after curfew when we went clubbing." She was whispering now. "And he smokes pot a lot. It's one of the things about him that I really hate."

Andrea sat silently, no expression on her face. Finally, she spoke. "I believe that someone is innocent until they're proven guilty. I'm not sure a drug test will be necessary, but I'm glad you're willing to take one."

Kelly nodded vigorously. "Absolutely."

"Here's what we're going to do. Tomorrow, you'll join in on activities during the day. You'll spend free time with me or Steve. And I'll have to talk to Dr. Wainwright. I don't know if he'll want you to go back to Rome or not."

"Has he called my parents again?" Kelly asked, her stomach clenching.

Andrea shook her head. "No, and I'm hoping that won't be necessary. Let's wait and see what happens tomorrow."

Kelly nodded, numbly. She was finally feeling like she belonged here, and now, abruptly, her visit might be over. And this time it wasn't even her fault. The injustice of it made her want to scream. She stood up and, at a total loss for words, went straight up to her room.

Marina was waiting at the door. "Spill it, right now."

With tears streaming down her face, Kelly told Marina about the e-mail. Marina listened silently, her face growing cloudier. "Joe. That little turd."

Kelly nodded miserably. "But he's a smart little turd. After everything I've done, Andrea and Dr. W will never believe I'm innocent."

Marina sighed. "You sure know how to pick 'em."

"Hey!"

"Right, sorry," Marina said. "The prodigal daughter has mended her ways. Well, at least Andrea said you were innocent until proven guilty."

"Do you really think she believes that?"

"Andrea's a little stiff, but she's a straight shooter, and she seems to like you. I don't think she'd b.s. you." Marina yawned. "Sadly, this melodrama won't resolve itself tonight. Wanna watch some tube?"

Kelly mustered up a half smile and shook her head. She climbed into bed, put her pillow over her head, and cried herself to sleep.

In the morning, Kelly watched helplessly as Andrea led Sheela out of the dining room for questioning.

"Sheela knows every idiotic thing I did this summer," she moaned to Marina. "I woke her up every time I came in after curfew. She could totally hang me out to dry right now." Kelly cradled her head in her hands.

Marina sighed impatiently. "Listen, anyone with half a brain can see that the only tripping you've ever done is on guilt. Are you inconsiderate? Affirmative. Bossy? I'd say. But Sheela knows you're not a druggie, and she'd never say you were."

"Yeah, but getting me out of her hair might be too big a temptation to resist," Kelly said miserably.

Before Marina could reply, Steve walked in and ushered

Rodney off to another room. This was turning into a full-scale inquisition.

"Wow, he looks even more petrified than you do," Marina said. She jumped out of her chair and headed off after them. "Nancy Drew is on the case. I'll let you know what I can overhear." She mock-saluted over her shoulder and was gone.

The next time Kelly saw Sheela and Marina was in the olive grove, where Signor Severino was giving a tour. The morning's activities had been a good distraction for Kelly, but the suspense was killing her—now that the three girls had a few minutes to talk, she needed to know what had gone on with Andrea.

She started with Sheela. "So what did you say?"

Sheela shrugged. "I told her about Starr's party."

Kelly racked her brain, trying to figure out what on earth the party could have to do with the drugs planted in her locker.

Sheela rolled her eyes. "It's so obvious, Kelly. We were at a party with absolutely no adult supervision and tons of booze and pot readily available. In four hours, I saw you take about three sips of punch and tell a stoner to take a hike. I thought that was pretty good evidence that you were innocent. Plus, everybody knows you're allergic to smoke. You haven't stopped complaining about it all summer."

Marina chuckled. "That's for sure. Just be glad you're not sitting next to her on the train."

Kelly turned to her. "Did you hear any of Steve's talk with Rodney?"

"You could say that. Rodney totally freaked out and spilled his guts. He told Steve that you guys went dancing and that Joe put crushed-up pills in the drinks. Apparently, Joe stole a bottle of tranquilizers from his mother before he left California. Rodney told Steve where he's hiding it. Rodney's being sent back to Rome for the rest of the trip. Dr. Wainwright wants to deal with him directly. I bet Joe will be, too."

Kelly was flabbergasted. "You overheard all that?"

"Nope." Marina smiled smugly. "I grabbed Rodney on the way out and asked him. There are advantages to looking like this, you know. Most guys are terrified of me."

Right now Kelly thought Marina was the most beautiful person she had ever seen. She shook her head, overcome by her friends' generosity. "You guys are the greatest. I totally don't deserve friends like you."

Sheela smiled at Marina. "She's not right often, but when she is, she's dead-on."

Signor Severino handed everyone a fresh olive, then laughed as they spat out the bitter fruit. "See? Not so delicious now. But when they are cured in brine or oil... *magnifico.*" He kissed his fingers and led them on to a nearby building, where he and Teresa pressed and bottled their own olive oil.

"Look, Sheela, they make oil especially for you," Marina whispered, grinning.

"Yeah, extra-virgin, I get it. You're hilarious," Sheela muttered back.

After they watched bushels and bushels of olives being transformed into thick, golden-green liquid, Signor Severino handed everyone a paper cup. "Taste it. It's the best way to know that you are getting a quality oil."

Kelly put a tiny drop of oil on her tongue, surprised by its rich, aromatic flavor. She added a bottle to the list of souvenirs she planned to bring home, then realized with a twinge that she might never get the opportunity. There was nothing she could do now; her fate was in Dr. Wainwright's hands.

In the afternoon, everyone walked into the nearby town to mail postcards and walk through its tiny, quaint streets. Kelly took in every last detail of the little village, savoring each new sight. If Dr. W's verdict was bad, she'd need some good memories to cling to over the next few days.

The call came right before dinner as a small group of kids sketched on the patio. Andrea jumped up quickly and walked out to the vegetable garden, speaking softly into her cell phone. Kelly and Marina strained their necks and

ears trying to catch any tidbits they could, but it was no use. Andrea was way too discreet.

When they saw her returning, both girls quickly returned to their drawings. "Kelly, can I have a word?" Andrea requested.

Kelly got up and followed her around the building, feeling as though she were heading straight into the jaws of the Bocca della Verità.

"I have good news. The details of your story match up with what several other students told us—we believe the pot isn't yours. For the time being, you're staying in the program."

Kelly couldn't help herself. She jumped up and down. "That's awesome! Thank you so much, Andrea!"

"Don't thank me, thank Dr. Wainwright. I'm just the messenger." Andrea put her hand on Kelly's shoulder. "There's more you should know. Steve spoke to Joe and Rodney this morning. Joe stonewalled him, but Rodney had a lot to say. I didn't tell you last night, but Dr. Wainwright didn't just find pot in your locker—there were a couple of pills, too.

"Rodney was really upset about what happened that night at the club. He told Steve that Joe was hiding a stash of drugs on campus. Besides a whole lot more pot and some alcohol, there was a bottle of prescription tranquilizers that matched up with the ones in your locker. I bet they're the same ones Joe put in your drinks that night.

Joe is on a train right now heading back to Rome. He's been expelled from the program."

Kelly stared at the ground. She didn't know what to say.

Andrea looked into Kelly's eyes. "Are you all right?"

Finally, she nodded. "I will be now. Thanks, Andrea."

Chapter Thirteen

The group stepped off the Circumvesuviana train promptly at eight-thirty the next morning. For the next two days, Kelly and the rest of the group would be touring Pompeii and Herculaneum. Now that Kelly wasn't in danger of getting kicked out of the program, she could really appreciate the sightseeing. And she had to admit, in the last few weeks, a little of Sheela's enthusiasm for Pompeii had rubbed off on her. She had her sketch pad ready as they entered the grounds.

Their guide, Gino, met them at the tourist office and, with a wink to the woman in the ticket booth, cut past the long line of tourists waiting for admission. Gino was an old friend of Dr. Wainwright's who worked at the Archaeological Museum in Naples. Because he had special privileges, he could show the kids places restricted to regular tourists. He was also taking them to the museum, where lots of artifacts from both cities were displayed. A fit, cheerful man in his fifties, Gino spoke excellent English and seemed to have a story about every pillar and paving stone in the city.

There were plenty of people inspecting the ruins, but walking the streets of Pompeii felt strangely lonely to Kelly. As she examined the brick outlines of shops, taverns, and homes that neighbored the gate to the city, it was painfully clear that this place was once a bustling center of business and culture. Then, on a normal August afternoon, the entire city was flattened by a mushroom cloud of volcanic ash as Mount Vesuvius erupted violently, twice.

Kelly looked up at the black mountain, framed by the columns of Pompeii's once-grand forum, and shuddered. She squinted at its peak, checking for any signs of activity. "Don't worry, Kel. It hasn't blown its top for sixty years. We'll probably make it through the week," Marina told her.

The stone streets, rutted by two-thousand-year-old wagon and chariot tracks, painted a rich picture of life in Pompeii.

"Don't tell me—they had swimming pools?" Kelly pointed into an elaborately landscaped courtyard.

"They had tons of modern conveniences," Sheela answered. "The richest citizens even had indoor plumbing, with toilet seats."

With every new building, arch, or fountain, Kelly learned something new about Pompeii's inhabitants. They came from all walks of life—filthy rich to penniless, aristocrat to slave. They ate fast food, worked out in the gym, took saunas at the spa. They had laundries, bakeries, candy stores, jewelry shops, bars, and even brothels. An open-air theater and sports arena provided all sorts of entertainment. Beautiful temples allowed them to worship Greek, Roman, and Egyptian deities.

Now all that was left were tourists and the stray dogs that everyone fed and petted, because legend had it they were the reincarnated victims of the lost city.

By lunchtime, Kelly was obsessed. She couldn't stop snapping photos. She was irritated by the students who complained about the heat or their aching feet.

Seeing the bodies was hard, though. Gino told them how, in the 1800s, an archaeologist digging in Pompeii discovered hollows in the hardened ash. He filled them with plaster, ending up with models of victims buried in the eruption. Over the centuries, their bodies had decomposed, leaving behind perfectly detailed molds. It was so eerie standing next to them, seeing the shock and pain on their faces, that Kelly's eyes filled with tears.

Behind her, Gino spoke softly. "The citizens of Pompeii

thought that the world was coming to an end. Imagine the sight—blazing ash raining down, the summer sky completely dark. A terrifying roar as a seemingly harmless mountain exploded upon them. Those of us who live near this place know to enjoy every moment of life. We have but to look toward Vesuvio for a reminder."

Kelly gazed at the dark form on the horizon, silhouetted against a pure blue backdrop. This place was so quiet, so strangely untouched. It was hard to fathom the horrors that had once taken place here. It was even harder to fathom that this incredible city had lain undiscovered for sixteen hundred years.

Sheela was right, as always. Visiting Pompeii was an experience Kelly would remember forever.

That night, Kelly sat at the wobbly desk in her cramped hotel room, scribbling and sketching every detail she could remember about Pompeii into her journal.

For once, she was looking forward to her reading assignment, two letters written by Pliny the Younger. The nephew of a famous general and historian who died in the eruption, the seventeen-year-old kid witnessed the mayhem from across the Bay of Naples. Years later, an important statesman himself, he wrote two letters describing the whole horrible event. According to Steve, those letters were still valuable references for volcanologists and historians today.

Marina had already finished them and was sitting on her bed, watching an Italian game show on TV and devouring a Toblerone bar. Every so often she let out a loud hoot, even though Kelly was pretty sure she didn't understand what was going on. A growing mound of balled-up papers littered the bedspread; Marina still hadn't found the perfect image for her tattoo.

Shutting her journal, Kelly realized she hadn't written to Starr in ages. Without much news to report about guys, hairstyles, or outfits, she couldn't think of much to say to her. Starr was fun, but the longer Kelly was away, the less she found herself thinking about her. Maybe Tyff was right; maybe this summer was changing her in more ways than she knew.

Kelly didn't want things to be different when she got back to suburban Chicago; she loved her life at home. She had pictured herself triumphantly returning to high school, an exotic, enchanting creature with a continental flair. Now she wondered if, instead, her friends at home would find her newfound interest in art and history dull and uncool. She glanced at Marina, who had abandoned her sketch pad and was plotting a new design on her ankle with a black marker. If the two of them could get along, anything was possible. Her real friends would love her, whoever she was.

• • •

Kelly had been standing in the museum gallery for who knows how long, staring and wondering how Marina would react. The fresco was a simple circle, painted on white plaster, but the resemblance was uncanny. The young woman gazed out at Kelly with soft brown eyes. She held a wax writing tablet in one hand, and with the other, she pressed a stylus thoughtfully against her lips. Her short brown curls were covered by a cap made of golden netting, and she had a cute gold hoop in each ear.

Kelly had only seen pictures of Marina's mom wearing jeans and a T-shirt, sitting on a motorcycle. But there was something about this face that was so familiar it sent a shiver up Kelly's back. She glanced over her shoulder; Marina was across the gallery, intently examining a slimy-looking serpent curling along the bottom of an otherwise beautiful fresco. Typical.

"'Rina, come here. You've got to see this." Reluctantly, Marina slouched over and looked. Her head snapped back and her eyes bulged.

"Holy shit. Yeah, you found it." Without moving her eyes, Marina reached out and gave Kelly a gentle slug in the arm. "Un-freakin'-believable. That's her." She pulled her digital camera out of her cargo pants and started snapping away. When she put the camera down, Kelly could swear her thick plum eyeliner was a little smudgier than usual.

Kelly ran to find Andrea. "Can Marina and I run down to the gift shop? There's a print I really want to buy her, and I don't want to forget."

Andrea nodded slowly. "Be back in fifteen minutes, okay? Otherwise I'll come looking for you."

"Ooh, scary," Marina whispered as they headed for the sweeping marble staircase. The Archaeological Museum had started life as a palace, but it was a perfect place to see art—huge, airy, and with gigantic windows that let in plenty of light. Each floor held another batch of treasures: paintings, sculpture, enormous carved cameos, even everyday objects rescued from the ruined cities.

In the bookstore, Marina showed the clerk the image on her camera. He nodded. "She is called *The Sappho of Pompeii*, because she was perhaps a poet. In ancient Rome, writing was a task often left to the women. We have prints in several sizes."

"It's a shame we don't know who painted it," Kelly murmured. Time and disaster had erased the identities of all the ancient artists. She looked into the poet's sweet face and sent a quick thank-you to its creator, whoever he or she was.

Marina made her choice and threw in a postcard of her favorite mosaic, an elaborate ocean-floor scene full of squid, fish, and other creepy-crawlies. She was virtually skipping as they headed back upstairs. Marina turned to Kelly, suddenly serious. "Thanks, Kel. I mean it. I'm not sure

I would have noticed her on my own. She's totally perfect. My mother even loved poetry; she read it all the time."

Kelly smiled. "That's what friends are for, right?"

Kelly sat on the train, a book about mosaics on her lap, gazing out the window. Now that they were on their way back to Rome, the landscape they passed was familiar and welcoming. Kelly only wished they'd had more time to explore some other little villages in Tuscany.

She was already planning a return trip to Italy; maybe she'd head up to Venice and finally see those gondolas. It sounded so romantic—canals winding through the city, an island where all they did was blow glass into beautiful objects, and the legendary Bridge of Sighs. She wondered if Luigi had ever been there.

Kelly's eyes popped open and she started rummaging through her bag. She hadn't checked her cell-phone messages for days—maybe he had finally called. She hit the "on" button and stared expectantly at the little window. Nothing. Kelly sank back into her seat. Maybe she had been too forward. Maybe he wanted to make the first move.

When she stepped off the metro at Circo Massimo, Kelly realized she was downright happy to see the old neighborhood again. And when they got back to school, Dr. Wainwright, with Signor and Signora Peretti at his side, was waiting for them in the driveway, grinning from ear to ear.

Some kids ran upstairs to unpack, and there was a traffic jam in the computer room, where kids had bolted to download their digital photos. Kelly decided to wait until later and headed for her room to finish studying her book and to recharge her phone.

Almost as soon as she plugged it into the outlet, it rang. Kelly jumped, then sighed. It was probably her parents, checking to make sure she had gotten back in one piece.

"Hello?"

"Is this Kelly Brandt?" The voice had a lilting Italian accent.

"Luigi!"

Sheela and Jarvis, who were cuddling on the common-room couch, leaned forward to listen. Kelly quickly shut the door on them.

"How are you?" Luigi asked. "Are you back from your travels?"

"I'm fine, thanks, and yes, about half an hour ago. We had an amazing time."

"I'm glad. But are you tired? Should I call you some other time?"

"No!" Oops. That sounded a little overeager. "I'm totally wired, so you picked a perfect time to call. What happened in Rome while I was away?"

Luigi laughed. "Wired is good, yes? I'm afraid for me, life has been quite dull. I am hoping you will entertain me with stories of your travels."

168

"Anytime," Kelly answered, positively beaming.

"Are you allowed to eat meals away from campus? May I take you out next Sunday? It is my day off from work."

"Absolutely. That would be great." They made plans to meet at three, in Parco Savello.

Kelly hung up the phone, flung open the door, and beamed at Sheela and Jarvis. Her own version of *Roman Holiday* was about to begin!

Kelly couldn't afford to get too distracted about her date— she had a mural to paint. For the final three weeks, the program had shifted gears. Classes were cut back to one hour each so that groups could form to select topics and begin their projects. At lunch one day, Sheela told Kelly and Marina about her project.

"Minnie and I are writing the autobiography of a Pompeiian teenager. We were inspired by this painting we saw in the museum in Naples." Sheela pulled a postcard out of her book bag. "She's called *Sappho of Pompeii.*"

Kelly and Marina stared, then laughed.

"You two are so alike, it's scary," Kelly told them. "Question is, which one of you is gonna start dressing like the other?"

When they had spoken on the phone earlier that day, Luigi had promised to lend Kelly some books about the Vatican. She figured that, worst-case scenario, she'd have an excuse to see him one more time after Sunday to return

them. In the meantime, Andrea was keeping her plenty busy.

"Don't be afraid to inject your personality into this project. I want you guys to have fun with this," Andrea told them.

The first chance she had, Kelly headed to Dr. Wainwright's office. He usually holed up there for a while after dinner. His door was ajar, so she tapped softly and poked her head in.

"Come on in, Kelly. What can I do for you?" Dr. Wainwright pushed his reading glasses onto his shiny forehead.

"For one thing, I never got to thank you for believing in me. I know things looked really bad, and I'm so grateful that you let me stay."

"That's very sweet of you, but in view of the evidence, I only did what was just."

Kelly nodded and turned to leave, but Dr. Wainwright called after her.

"I almost forgot." He opened a desk drawer and began rummaging through it. Finally, he pulled out a small envelope. "I found this when I was conducting my unfortunate investigation of your locker. It was wedged into a ridge in the corner and was quite well hidden. Is it yours?"

Kelly opened the envelope.

"My locket!" She had rushed downstairs to rummage for

an outfit right before she and Joe had gone clubbing. It must have fallen off then.

"The clasp was a little loose," Dr. Wainright said, "so I did a bit of surgery on it. It should be quite secure now." He smiled. "I'm glad you have it back, and I'm glad you made it back to Rome with us."

"I am, too. More than you can imagine."

Kelly fastened the chain around her neck, and let the warm metal rest over her heart. Once again, she had a phone call to make to her parents. And this time, she couldn't wait.

Chapter Fourteen

To: kelcat@email.com
From: m&ebrandt@email.com
Subject: The locket

Hi honey,

Dad and I got your message when we got back from the lake yesterday. I'm so thrilled that you found the locket. And your art teacher, Andrea, sent us a lovely note telling us what great progress you're making on your mural project. We're glad to hear you're working hard. Take a picture of it for us when it's finished, okay? We can't wait to see you in just a few short weeks. Your father definitely could use your advice on his tie choices these days.

Love,
Mom

Kelly stood on a ladder holding a huge sheet of paper, calculating how much space she needed for her Vatican painting. It was important to get this settled first so that nobody became a wall hog. Luckily, Veronica's Egyptian obelisk was tall and skinny, which left more room for the other five.

Kelly shook the charcoal dust out of her hair. She desperately needed to start her predate overhaul. *One hour and forty-five minutes until Operation Luigi. Wash hair. Clean under nails. Shave legs and pits. Moisturize!* The whole shebang would take at least an hour.

With a meter stick, she measured out a decent-looking block and held up her rough sketch. She marked her turf, then hopped down and helped Marina move the ladder over to her spot. Her work here was done. Kelly slapped the dust off herself and bolted, waving over her shoulder at the rest of the group.

"Give him hell, Kel!" Marina bellowed.

She hadn't felt this excited—or nervous—in ages. But when Kelly stepped through the park gate at five minutes

after three, she looked cool and collected in Sheela's beaded Indian skirt (borrowed—with permission!) and a white sleeveless blouse. She found Luigi sitting on a bench reading a paperback.

"A pleasure to see you again, signorina." He bowed and touched his lips to the back of her hand. "*Allora,* I am at your disposal. What would you like to do this afternoon?"

"Oh, anything, really. I'm just happy to spend some time with a charming Italian gentleman." Kelly peeked up at him through her lashes and smiled.

Luigi laughed good-naturedly. "Well, let me know when you find him. In the meantime, I am happy to show you around." He paused, looking over the hills and thinking. "I'm sure you've already seen it—the keyhole?"

Kelly didn't have a clue what he meant. "Um, I don't know."

"Ah, come with me. I'll show you a very special treasure of Aventino." They left the orange-scented *parco* and headed up Via di Santa Sabina. The street ended in a little piazza surrounded by white walls decorated with obelisks and statues.

"This building is home to the Knights of Malta, a religious order. The artist Piranesi designed this place for them."

Kelly nodded. She had heard of Piranesi, but still didn't understand why they were there. Luigi led her over to one

174

of several doors in the wall. A few tourists milled around, waiting, as people pressed their faces against it. When it was their turn, Luigi put his hand on her shoulder. "Tell me what you see."

Kelly peeked through the brass keyhole and laughed. Piranesi had created a tiny work of art by positioning a simple keyhole in just the right place. The view, perfectly framed by an arch of leafy trees, was of the glimmering dome of the Vatican. "That's pretty cool, I must admit."

"If you ever need inspiration for your mural, you have only to walk here and take a look."

They walked back toward the park, chatting up a storm. Soon Luigi stopped next to a Vespa and unlocked it, handing Kelly a helmet. "I was thinking we could have dinner in Trastevere. How does that sound?"

"Great," Kelly answered, staring at the scooter. It was pretty high up on her parents' list of no-nos. *Thou shalt stay off scooters.* But what the hell? She put on the helmet and climbed on, wrapping her arms tightly around Luigi's waist.

She had been to Trastevere a couple of times, but it was nicer with Luigi. He showed her quaint back alleyways crowded with dusty little shops, including a great English-language bookshop, where Kelly picked up a couple of novels for the flight home. Next they followed the Passeggiata del Gianicolo to the top of Janiculum hill,

where they were rewarded with a staggering view of the city. Over espressos, they talked and watched kids riding the merry-go-round.

Later, they ate dinner outside, next to a bubbling fountain, at a romantic little trattoria. Kelly told Luigi about her life at home—her parents, her friends, and all the activities she was involved with at school. Luigi told her about his family, college life, and his summer job at the Vatican.

"I get to meet interesting people from all over," he said. "And once in a while, I can help a beautiful, lost stranger. That's the best part of my job."

"I hope that doesn't mean you're having dinner with every girl who asks you for help," Kelly said teasingly.

"Don't worry." Luigi laughed. "You are one of a kind."

For dessert, Luigi took her for the best gelato of the entire trip. Much sooner than Kelly wanted, she and Luigi were saying good night on the front steps of the PIR.

"How much longer before you go home?"

"Just over two weeks." The thought nearly broke Kelly's heart.

"May I see you again before then?"

"I'd love that."

Luigi kissed her, first on one cheek, then on the other, and again on the opposite side. In return, Kelly gave him a big, American-style hug. Grinning, Luigi hopped on his scooter and roared off into the most perfect evening ever.

• • •

"What time is that thing later?" Marina asked Kelly.

"Eightish, I think. Sheela is a train wreck, she's so nervous."

The girls were in the cafeteria, finishing the outlines of their buildings. In the week since they'd returned to Rome, everyone had made good progress on the mural. Andrea had started things off for them by priming the wall and painting it the piercing blue of the Roman sky. Then she added some cottony clouds and, among them, a pair of round-faced cherubs. The room looked brighter and happier already.

"Do you know what Orations are, exactly?" Kelly asked.

Marina scratched her nose, leaving a big, black paint streak. "From what I can tell, they put on togas, go to the Forum, and read famous speeches in Latin. Y'know, standing in the original guys' footprints and whatnot."

It sounded even more boring than Kelly had thought, but it meant so much to Sheela, she wanted to be there for her.

"C'mon, it'll be cute watching the brainiacs put on a show. Is sweetie pie coming?" Marina teased.

Kelly had been taking every opportunity to spend time with Luigi, in person and on the phone. The idea of the Forum, lit up by a gorgeous sunset with the lights of the city glimmering behind it, was too romantic to pass up. "Yes, and he's taking me out to dinner first."

Marina snorted. "I'd bet you've already got your Italian

couture wedding dress all picked out. You better let me know when you set the date. I know a guy who makes great skirts out of old seat belts, but they're made to order."

Before Luigi picked her up, Kelly ran to the local flower shop and talked the clerk into making her a garland of laurel leaves. Sheela deserved a prize for facing up to her fear of public speaking; strange how something so harrowing for poor Sheela came so effortlessly to Kelly.

By six o'clock, Kelly was primped, polished, and standing on the steps of the PIR as Luigi drove up. *Right on time,* Kelly thought. *And he looks adorable on that Vespa.*

Luigi smiled as he got off the bike and kissed Kelly hello.

"Ciao." Kelly beamed. "Thanks for coming."

"It is my pleasure, signorina," Luigi answered, handing Kelly his spare helmet and getting back on the Vespa. "Come, your chariot awaits you."

Kelly climbed on and slid her arms snugly around Luigi. She could definitely get used to this.

Kelly had no idea what "Sott'er cielo de Roma" meant, but the song certainly sounded romantic. She and Luigi were sitting across from each other at a small table at La Cisterna, the oldest restaurant in Trastevere. As far as Kelly was concerned, this was already the best date she had ever been on. Luigi was so sweet and charming, he made her feel like a Roman goddess. And after an unspeakably delicious pasta dinner, the two of them were being serenaded by a tuxedo-clad tenor. When he finished, everyone applauded loudly. The man smiled broadly and winked at Kelly before he moved on to another table.

"This is perfect," Kelly gushed. "The restaurant is beautiful, the dinner was beautiful—"

"And you are beautiful," Luigi finished, blushing despite himself. "But I have one more treat for you before we go to the Forum."

Luigi helped Kelly out of her seat, then led her down to the restaurant's lower level. Kelly picked her way over the cobblestones, careful not to get her stilettos stuck. Luigi stopped in front of what looked like some kind of well. "La Cisterna is named for this," he explained in a soft voice. "It's an ancient well from imperial times."

Pulling her close, Luigi reached into his pocket and pulled out a silver coin.

"Legend says that if you toss a coin into the well, your wish will go straight into the heart of Rome, and will surely come true." He pressed the coin into Kelly's hand and kissed her gently on the lips.

Kelly closed her eyes, tossed the coin over her shoulder, and wished for another summer in Rome.

As predicted, sunset at the Forum was spectacular; the ruins were bathed in soft, orange light and the sky was

streaked with pinks and purples. Kelly and Luigi met up with Marina in front of the Senate Building to watch the orators' procession. Kelly noted with pleasure that Luigi didn't even blink over Marina's offbeat appearance.

About twenty students and a few curious bystanders milled around in front of a low stone column called the Umbilicus Mundus, which sounded to Kelly like it meant "belly button of the world." Crazy Romans.

Six kids, including Sheela and Jarvis, arrived in togas and sandals, carrying rolled paper scrolls. Dr. Wainwright, and Marco, also wearing robes, led them to the Rostra, the ancient stone platform where the empire's greatest speakers had voiced their opinions.

"You know, after he had the famous orator Cicero assassinated, Marc Anthony ordered his head and hands cut off and nailed to the Rostra for all Romans to see," Luigi whispered.

"Nice," Marina said. "Don't tell Sheela till afterward."

Dr. Wainwright delivered a brief, official-sounding speech in Latin, and then turned the platform over to Jarvis. With dignity and poise, holding his tall, scrawny body rod-straight, Jarvis opened his mouth and delivered a five-minute-long string of pure gibberish. Worst of all, when he finished, he repeated his speech in English—and it still made no sense to Kelly.

By speaker number three, Kelly had stroked Luigi's hand a hundred and forty-seven times, counted thirty-nine airplanes landing at Fiumicino Airport, and completely lost interest in Orations. But when Sheela's turn came, she forced herself to focus. The poor girl looked petrified; even in the semidarkness, Kelly could see the scroll shaking in her hands. But her voice was clear and expressive and her delivery was dramatic and convincing. Kelly caught her eye and smiled encouragingly.

Soon Sheela had completed the Latin and was moving on to the English translation. "'On Friendship,'" she said, "by Marcus Tullius Cicero.

"'The most difficult thing in the world is for a friendship to remain unimpaired to the end of life. So many things might intervene: conflicting interests; differences of opinion in politics; frequent changes in character.'" As she spoke, her eyes moved from Kelly to Jarvis to Marina, Lisa, and Minnie. "'Let this, then, be laid down as the first law of friendship, that we should ask from friends, and do for friends, only what is good. But do not let us wait to be asked either...Let us have the courage to give advice with candor.'"

Kelly blushed as she remembered all the times Sheela had stuck up for her, stuck out her neck for her, and told her when she was being a jerk.

"'How can a life be worth living,'" Sheela continued, "'which lacks that repose which is to be found in the mutual goodwill of a friend? What can be more delightful than to have someone to whom you can say everything

with the same absolute confidence as to yourself?'" She smiled out at the audience, and paused before the last line. "'The greatest of all things is Friendship.'"

Kelly agreed with every word—the luckiest people were the ones who had friends. Flawed, honest, true-blue friends.

When the last words echoed through the Forum, the audience erupted in cheers. Kelly ran up to the platform and placed the leaf garland on Sheela's head.

"Thank you for being my friend," she whispered.

Chapter Fifteen

There were only ten days left; ten days to finish projects, spend time with friends, and soak up every last drop of Rome. Kelly had painted the entire Vatican on the wall; now all she had to do was add about three million details. Lunch was winding up, and she could hear plates and silverware clattering and kids chatting behind the makeshift curtain that hid the mural wall. Dr. Wainwright wanted the finished product to be a surprise.

Knowing there was so little time left brought everyone closer. Even Lisa, who generally avoided Kelly like the plague, had become slightly more civil. And Minnie was

positively genial since Kelly had rescued her in Siena. One night, sitting in the common room, Kelly realized that she'd miss hearing *Aïda* three times a day. She'd even miss old Lisa, who had taught her volumes about ozone-friendly hairspray.

Several other groups were using the cafeteria as their workroom. A big cardboard model of Florence's Duomo and an ancient Roman cookbook were coming together on one of the long tables. Several other kids were taking a study break, playing Boggle in Italian.

In three months, this place had become home. Kelly would never have believed it, but it was true. She didn't even mind the heat so much anymore.

As each hour went by, another pillar, another statue, another window appeared on the Vatican. Kelly put down her paintbrush and checked her watch: 3:51. Luigi had asked her to meet him at the Vatican at 4:30; he wouldn't say why. She cleaned the paint off her hands and arms in the huge kitchen sink and hustled off to the metro station. These days, time was at a premium, and as much as she loved being with Luigi, the mural wasn't painting itself.

Still, as she entered the information center, Kelly felt warm and nostalgic. Luigi was in his usual place behind the desk, telling two old ladies where to find the closest bathroom. When she walked in, he smiled—the same mischievous grin that had cheered her up the first time they met.

After a few minutes, Luigi joined her on the other side

of the desk. "I got permission to leave work early today. I explained that I had something very important to do."

He led her across St. Peter's Square to the Basilica, which Kelly had missed on her first visit. He flashed his ID and spoke rapidly to the guards at the door, who, with a wink to Kelly, waved them inside. They weren't nearly as intimidating this time around.

"I know you didn't get to go inside when you were here before," Luigi said, taking her hand. "How would you like a guided tour?"

The Basilica was enormous, and beautiful. Kelly stared up at the elaborately carved altar, supported by four ornate golden columns. "The great sculptor Bernini designed the high altar," Luigi told her. "Only the pope is permitted to give mass here. It stands over the spot where many believe Saint Peter, the first pope, is buried."

There were ornamental carvings everywhere Kelly looked. And the columns she had admired were solid gold. Just like the galleries, this place housed a treasure trove of magnificent artwork.

"There are no paintings in the Basilica," Luigi explained. "Only mosaics. It is necessary to constantly repair and maintain these works, and to create new ones, as well."

Kelly turned her attention to a marble statue sitting in a huge glass case. "Michelangelo, right? We studied the *Pietà* in art class."

"You're correct. Did you know it is the only work that

bears his signature?" Luigi pointed to the sash running over the Virgin Mary's shoulder.

They spent nearly an hour in the Basilica, then Luigi grabbed Kelly's arm. "There's one more place I'd like to take you before closing. I think you'll enjoy seeing it."

It was a workshop, off the beaten tourist path. "Here we have our own mosaic artists working full-time to keep St. Peter's beautiful," Luigi whispered.

Kelly watched the men bent intently over their work. The mosaic tiles were tiny and delicate. Micromosaic, Luigi called it. Rome was a bustling, chaotic city. But in this peaceful place, artists toiled away all day, with tweezers and magnifying glasses, piecing together intricate works of art one tiny stone shard at a time.

"I guess my project isn't as overwhelming as I thought," Kelly said.

As they walked back through Piazza San Pietro, Kelly gave Luigi a kiss on the cheek. "This has given me loads of inspiration for the mural. Thank you so much for doing this for me. But I've really got to get back to work."

"May I come see it?"

"If you promise you won't laugh. I'm not the greatest painter."

Kelly felt a bit nervous introducing Luigi to the mural group, especially to Andrea. She had become genuinely fond of the five other kids—in the many hours they'd spent together, the motley group had formed a bond. And Andrea? She was the cool older sister Kelly wished she had.

Andrea and Luigi had a nice conversation in Italian—Kelly couldn't understand all of it, but she could tell that they were saying nice things about her. Watching them talk, with Marina working in the background, brought a lump to her throat. She would miss them so badly it hurt.

"But you lied to me!" Luigi told her as he surveyed her work. "You are a wonderful painter."

Luigi kept her company until dinnertime, then Kelly walked him to his Vespa. "I have one more surprise for you," he said. "I hope you will think it's a pleasant one."

Kelly's heart began to pound.

"I will be visiting America in about three months' time. Is Chicago very far from New York City? My friends and I decided several months ago to travel there for our winter holiday."

"It's about a thousand miles." She looked up at him thoughtfully. "You know, Chicago has some really important architecture. There are all these great old office buildings, Navy Pier, and just outside the city there are some amazing Frank Lloyd Wright houses. No engineering student should miss it."

Luigi laughed. "I will consider that very seriously, Professor."

She kissed Luigi good night and rushed back to her work in the caf, wondering how her parents would like spending Christmas break in New York City.

Kelly weeded through her half of the dresser, figuring out what to wear for her last three days in Rome. There was so much left to do! She pulled out a drawer and dumped the contents into a garbage bag—she'd lug it down to her storage space later. She had a summer's worth of shopping to do this afternoon—gifts for everybody, plus a couple of souvenirs for herself.

The night before, she had put the final strokes of paint onto her Vatican. Before hitting the shops, Kelly ran downstairs for one last look. St. Peter's stood shoulder to shoulder with Marina's boldly stroked, brashly colored PIR building. Veronica's obelisk sat in the center, with Dai's crazily intricate rendering of the Colosseum next to it. On the opposite end, Hildy's Fountain of Trevi kept company with Gaby's perfectly rendered Pantheon.

Kelly surveyed her own work critically. It was decent. And it had been fun to paint. For laughs, she had placed two superserious Swiss Guards at the entrance to the Basilica, holding traditional long-handled axes. But at the top of one, instead of a sharp metal blade, flew a white flag. On it she painted a tiny yellow tank top and a pair of pink shorts, with a bright red slash drawn through them. On the left side of the piazza, a tall, thin young man with glasses smilingly offered brochures to camera-toting tourists.

Looking more closely at Marina's painting, she found a tiny Kelly and Sheela, waving from their fourth-floor window. Two stories down, Dr. Wainwright stood on the terrace outside his office. Marina had signed her name in flowing graffiti script.

The next morning was open house. Everyone's projects would be displayed, read, or performed. The kids who lived in Rome were invited to bring their families. Luigi had promised to stop by on his lunch break. The banquet would take place afterward.

As Kelly stood in front of the mural, deep in thought, Andrea appeared next to her. "You guys did an amazing job. I'm really proud of you." She looked at Kelly in her usual thoughtful way. "You know, you should really consider majoring in art at college. Dr. Wainwright and I meant what we said—you're genuinely talented."

Kelly had always been more concerned with where she'd go to college than with what she'd study. She had wanted to go to a city that had an active nightlife, maybe New York City or Los Angeles. She'd just assumed she'd work the rest out later. "You can do that? For college credit?"

Andrea laughed. "It worked for me. You have to take other courses, too, but art counts just as much as any other major. If you'd like, I'll get you some information about some good programs back home."

Kelly nodded. "I would love that." She felt her eyes beginning to dampen. "Thanks, Andrea. For everything."

"It's my pleasure, Kelly. This summer would have been dull without you."

The two of them stood in companionable silence, admiring the mural.

Chapter Sixteen

The presents sat in Kelly's backpack, neatly wrapped in pretty paper bags sealed with little ribbons. Two copies of *Italian Vogue* were tucked in her suitcase, one for Tyff, one for Starr. And a spanking-new, hotter-than-hell leather jacket was burning a hole in her suitcase, far from Lisa's disapproving eyes.

The library was jam-packed with the fruits of everybody's labor. The projects ranged from a huge wooden model of an ancient Roman ship to Kelly's favorite, a modern-day Italian traffic-survival guide.

Parents and students swarmed the building, speaking in

a dozen different languages and making a fuss over the projects. Kelly felt like a proud mother as she stood by the mural, answering questions and having her picture taken. She only wished her own parents could be there, to meet her friends and see how far she'd come.

After the day-schoolers and their parents went home, a group of summer kids sat on the roof terrace, drinking Cokes, trading project horror stories, and just talking. In the yard below them, a few students juggled a soccer ball in the waning afternoon sunshine. Kelly shut her eyes and breathed deep, smelling the odd mix of orange blossoms, diesel exhaust, and warm earth that she'd come to know and love in Aventino.

At six, everyone ran upstairs to get dressed for the program's farewell banquet. Kelly and Sheela primped in front of their tiny mirror, fixing each other's hair and dancing to cheesy Euro pop blasting from Sheela's clock radio. Marina met them downstairs in her party outfit—a miniskirt made out of black electrical tape, a black bat-wing top, and platform boots. "And you guys thought I never dressed up," she said, spinning.

The banquet was held at the same *osteria* where they'd eaten their first dinner in Rome. This time, the simple wood tables were decked out with candles, linen tablecloths, and bottles of wine. Best of all, they were serving one of Kelly's favorite dishes, risotto.

Kelly had grown to love the creamy rice dish while she

was in Italy, though this one looked a little strange to her. She was picking out the little black specks scattered over the top when Sheela elbowed her in the ribs. "Don't you like truffles?"

Kelly shrugged. "I don't know. I haven't tasted it yet. I'm trying to get rid of the burned stuff first."

"No, dummy. That's truffle. Try it, it's good. And too expensive to waste."

Kelly took a bite. She couldn't describe the taste, but she liked it. Kind of mushroomy, but with other flavors she couldn't identify. "That's insanely yummy. Can you get these at home?"

"You can, but I think they cost a lot more there." Sheela put a forkful into her mouth and shut her eyes. "We should go halfies on a bottle of truffle oil or something before we leave. This is heavenly."

"You'll enjoy this," Dr. Wainwright announced as a dish holding a round brown blob was put in front of each diner. "*Tartufo*—ice cream, smothered in shaved chocolate and whipped cream, with a sour cherry in the center. It's named after the treat you just finished, the truffle, because of its resemblance to the little fungus."

"Oh, that's appetizing," Marina groused. "Now I feel like I ate athlete's foot for dinner."

"It could be worse," Jarvis answered. "You could have eaten jock itch." Kelly and Sheela exchanged looks and giggled.

When every bit of chocolate had been licked from every spoon, Dr. Wainwright stood up, tapping his wineglass for silence. His rumpled pinstripe suit made him look even more professorial than usual.

"Friends, Romans, countrymen and women—lend me your ears. I am blessed to be an educator. In what other profession is one surrounded by enthusiastic, fascinating, intelligent, young people? Not only do I get to do what I love—teach—I learn from my students every day.

"Whenever I say farewell to a group of students, my heart aches, because I will miss each and every one of you. But my heart also sings, because I know that you are leaving here enriched, empowered, and invigorated by your experiences in this program. It gives me hope, knowing that you youngsters are our future. Thank you for a lovely summer."

Dr. Wainwright smiled. "Now please join me in thanking our superlative instructors." He waved a long arm down the length of the table, and the kids broke out in cheers. Waving and smiling, the teachers stood, some taking mock bows. When the noise died down, Marco jumped from his seat and shouted, *"A Dottore Wainwright! Mille grazie! Salute!"*

Everyone stood and toasted Dr. Wainwright's very good health. And to a job very well done.

Later, the group gathered in the lounge. Andrea and Steve had put together a slide show of pictures taken on their road trip. Kelly winced when Joe's face flashed by, but she loved the shots of herself mugging for the camera with Marina and Sheela. And the pictures of Siena made her smile. Despite everything, it had been a wonderful trip.

Afterward, everyone stayed up way too late, hugging, exchanging info, and packing. As Kelly soaked in the frenzied mood, she realized that something was missing. She found Marina sitting alone in her room, hunkered down over a pad full of drawings.

Marina raised an eyebrow at her. "What can I do for you, Brandt?"

"I need to take a break from packing. Mind if I hang out awhile?"

The two girls talked into the early hours. Marina promised to send Kelly photos when her tattoo was finished. Kelly promised to send Marina a T-shirt (in black, naturally) from Second City, the improv comedy theater in Chicago. Marina even posed for a photo, sticking out her studded tongue and making devil's horns with both hands. She refused to say good-bye.

"No gooey stuff, Brandt. We'll be talking in a couple days. You'll just have to take my abuse via e-mail."

In the morning, the same little buses that had brought them to the PIR at the beginning of the summer appeared in the driveway again. Luigi pulled up on his Vespa—he had made a special trip to Aventino to say good-bye—and

the whole PIR staff stood outside, checking tickets and passports.

Marco kissed everyone on both cheeks, including the boys. Steve gave them each a rib-crushing bear hug.

Kelly felt almost shy saying good-bye to Andrea. She wanted to tell her so many things—how much she admired her, how much she appreciated the faith Andrea had in her, how much she would miss her—but she found herself at a rare loss for words. "You're a great teacher," she finally managed.

Andrea smiled warmly. "Don't forget to e-mail me, okay? I want to know how AP art is going. And if you find yourself in Boston, I hope you'll visit me. We can go to the Gardner Museum, or maybe do some shopping on Newbury Street." Andrea was finishing her Ph.D. work at Harvard. Kelly nodded, knowing that if she opened her mouth again, a sob would burst out.

Dr. Wainwright fixed his sparkling eyes on Kelly and gripped her hand tightly. "Young lady, you are a joy. I'm absolutely certain that whatever you choose to do with your life, you'll be a tremendous success."

Kelly answered him with a tearful hug.

Then she took a deep breath and walked over to Luigi. He had been waiting patiently while she bid her teachers farewell, and smiled as she walked toward him.

"Luigi," Kelly started, "I want to tell you how much I . . ." She couldn't put into words what she needed him to know.

When it came to flirting, or getting boys to fall for her, Kelly was unstoppable. But this was uncharted territory. She had no idea how to say good-bye to someone she cared for so much. She swallowed hard, avoiding his warm eyes.

Luigi reached out and tucked a stray hair behind her ear. He gently took her hands in his and smiled sadly. "I'll miss you, Kelly Brandt. And Roma will miss you."

Kelly blinked back tears. "Same here," she replied.

Luigi held her tightly, and with a quaver in his voice, he whispered in her ear, *"Ciao, bella."*

As they kissed, Kelly wished that time would stand still. Reluctantly, she turned and got on the bus. She watched as Luigi, her beloved school, and her beloved neighborhood faded into the distance.

The flight was perfectly smooth, but Kelly couldn't fall asleep. Her brain was buzzing and her heart was bursting with emotion. There was no way she could ever express how she was feeling, but she needed to try. Pulling her notebook out of her backpack, she began writing. First came Dr. Wainwright. Andrea was next, and then Marina. The final letter was to Luigi.

Once in a while a tear splatted the lined paper, but Kelly didn't care. The words kept tumbling out, page after page. When she finished, she was utterly exhausted, and slept until the plane touched down at O'Hare Airport. There was no time to fix her makeup, but Kelly didn't care so much.

She was a lot more than a pretty face; she knew that now.

At the same gate where they had arrived, Kelly stood patiently as Sheela and Jarvis clung to each other, whispering their farewells. Reluctantly, Kelly put her hand on her friend's shoulder. Jarvis had a connecting flight to catch and their families were waiting for them.

"Andrea told me that Carnegie Mellon in Pittsburgh has a fantastic art program. That's where Jarvis is from, right?"

"Right," Sheela said, smiling and wiping her eyes.

"You know, before the weather gets too cold we should take a road trip. We could check out some schools and visit Jarvis, too. I think it's about time I started working on getting some wheels, don't you?"

Sheela shook her head. "You're not driving all the way to Pittsburgh. Do you know how many speeding tickets we'll get? I'm driving."

"No way, slowpoke. Besides, who's better than me at talking her way out of speeding tickets? I'm driving."

"It's settled, then," Sheela said drily. "We'll take the train."

Arm in arm, the two girls headed down the long hallway, getting closer to home with every step. The afternoon sun streamed through the windows, glinting off the wings of planes arriving from all over the world. One journey was ending, but Kelly knew there would be many more. To college, into adulthood, and anywhere else *la dolce vita* wanted to take her. She was ready to jump in, whooping and hollering all the way.

Turn the page for a special preview of another

novel:

Westminster
Abby

Chapter One

"In the event of an emergency, a member of the flight crew shall direct you to the nearest exit."

Abby Capshaw shifted nervously in the narrow confines of her tiny window seat. One of these days, she vowed to herself, when she was long past high school and making an actual salary instead of a paltry allowance and some money from babysitting, she was going to spring for a first-class ride. The plane had taken off, like, three seconds ago, and already her knees were cramping.

Normally Abby would be paying attention to the announcements that the captain was making over the

loudspeaker, or craning her neck to see the flight crew's safety demonstration. She was a firm believer that one never could be too cautious—she'd seen *Castaway*. It was important to be prepared. And Abby was nothing if not the responsible type. She was spacing now for two very specific reasons.

For starters, she couldn't understand a word that the captain was saying. She knew he was speaking in English because this was a British Airways flight and, well, he *was* English, but she had quickly discovered—with no small amount of dismay—that apparently a British accent was actually kind of tough to decipher in any context other than a Hugh Grant movie. Since boarding Flight 0178 to London's Heathrow Airport, Abby had found herself doing more politely ambiguous nodding than she had, pretty much, ever done in her whole life (family reunions notwithstanding).

So listening to the captain was essentially an exercise in futility. Though she did note with some amusement that he pronounced *direct* as "die-rect."

Just like Hugh Grant. Mmmm...

The other reason that Abby was slightly less concerned than usual about hearing the announcements had to do with why she was on this plane to begin with: the whole "responsible type" thing. As in, she was tired of it. And she was looking for a change. Starting now.

Abby's junior year of high school had begun with a vow:

Things were going to be different this year. Last fall, on September 13, Abby had turned sixteen. She was a Virgo. Normally she didn't pay all that much attention to things like horoscopes and the zodiac, but her best friend, Dani Schumacher, was a huge believer in it, and, as such, kept Abby well informed on the subject.

According to *Who Do the Stars Think You Are?* (a dubious source, in Abby's humble opinion), being a Virgo meant that Abby was "a hardworking, dedicated personality who wants perfection in all you do. Because you are very organized, you make the perfect party planner!"

In other words, totally boring. (Except for that party-planner thing, which didn't so much apply to her life. Though one time her principal asked her to put together a casual going-away thing for her English teacher. But there was nothing sexy about a party your principal asked you to plan.)

Abby had to admit to herself that life in New York City was pretty much okay. She went to a nice private school where the kids were decent and down-to-earth, even though most of them had a lot of money—definitely more money than she had (well, technically, more than her parents). She got very good grades and tutored through a peer-to-peer program. She had a small, close-knit circle of friends. Maybe she wasn't captain of the cheerleading squad or anything like that, but she fit in and felt well liked.

Terminally boring.

She had discovered that she was a little vanilla. Actually, way more than a little. She needed some flavor. Some hot fudge or colored sprinkles. Ideally, she could spin "vanilla" into "hot fudge sundae." The goal had been to put the plan into action over the course of junior year. But things hadn't quite worked out the way Abby'd planned.

Her parents were completely overprotective of her (not that she'd ever given them reason to be—so unfair), making her stay home most Friday nights for "family time" and forbidding her to date until she was seventeen. Seventeen was ancient. Seventeen was *senior* year. By then, everyone in school would have paired off and she'd be lucky to go to the prom with her cousin Jeff. Clearly that was out of the question. Things had to change, and fast.

"Biscuits?"

Abby felt a tap at her arm and looked up to see a cheery blond flight attendant beaming away at her. "Huh?" she asked.

"Biscuits, luv. A package."

Abby peered at the plastic package, trying to decipher what was inside. It was definitely something of the edible variety, that much was for sure, but as a general rule, she liked to have a vague sense of what she was eating before she dove in. Then again, she *was* sort of hungry. She nodded and took the snack. If nothing else, it was a crash course in British culture.

4

"Something to drink?"

Abby shrugged. "Water?"

"Certainly. Fizzy or still?"

"Um... tap. Plain. I mean, still," Abby stammered. The flight attendant passed a small chilled bottle across the row. Abby took her drink and placed it down on her tray, then ripped open the package of biscuits.

Oh! Biscuits were cookies. These were plain and flat, and cream-colored, probably vanilla-flavored. Not very exciting. Kind of like Abby's life. How appropriate.

She mentally flipped through the glossary she'd been sent from her program director before leaving: *bird, biscuit, bloke, boot, brolly, chemist, jumper, knickers, lorry, loo, newsagent, pants, trainers, WC*—the words were either completely foreign, or familiar, but with a totally different meaning. For instance, she'd been warned not to use the word *pants* to mean "trousers" because in England, pants were underwear. Like *knickers.* Knickers were also under-wear. Totally confusing.

Abby didn't care—that much—though, because being in this cramped, crowded plane and navigating her way through secret, coded language and pseudoexotic snacks was the first step toward that hot-fudge-sundae lifestyle she so craved. She was on her way to London. To *live.*

A thrill ran through her just thinking about it. She'd been accepted to the S.A.S.S. program—a program that encouraged high-school girls to study abroad—then she'd

been approved for admittance to City College, a university based in the eastern area of the city, for a ten-week summer session. Ten weeks. In London, one of the most cosmopolitan cities in the world. London was all about cool, sophisticated accents, fancy meals like "high tea," live theater that rivaled Broadway, actual royalty complete with palaces and everything—and she'd be right in the middle of it.

Was she scared? No way.

She was terrified.

The most ironic part about the trip was that the whole thing had been her parents' idea in the first place. *They* had been the ones who'd found the S.A.S.S. program and decided that it sounded like "an opportunity not to be missed." *They* had been the ones who *insisted* that Abby apply. The same people who got on Abby when she received an A-minus rather than an A on a paper or a test (which for the record, was pretty damn rare). The same people who acted shocked when Abby professed a desire to see a movie with her friends rather than play Boggle on family night. It was these two people who had driven Abby to elaborate measures of faux rebellion such as talking on her phone from inside her bedroom closet when it was later than 10 P.M., her "phone curfew." *Those people* actually *wanted her to move to England. For ten whole weeks.*

Ultimately, Abby's reasons for wanting to stay and her parents' *highly* uncharacteristic reasons for wanting to

6

ship her off to a different time zone were one and the same. One reason, to be precise. A boy reason.

A boy named James.

Back in November, Abby would have given anything not to be separated from James, which was obviously why her parents had insisted on doing just that. They pulled out that "not until you're seventeen" bull, which Abby was pretty sure they'd made up on the spot just because she'd happened to take an interest in the opposite sex. She was too young to date, they proclaimed, but paradoxically, she was old enough to be thrown to the proverbial wolves for the summer. The British wolves.

Abby had used every tactic she could possibly conceive of: She cried, begged, pleaded, suffered weeks without talking to her parents or eating (in their presence, anyway)...to no effect. Abby loved James, James was bad news, Abby was going to England.

At the eleventh hour, Abby had finally come to terms with the tragic situation and used her rather prodigious babysitting savings to buy James a plane ticket over to England to visit her halfway through the summer term. There was *no way* that she was going to spend the entire summer apart from the boy she loved.

It was funny how things could change so dramatically, so quickly, Abby thought.

She took a sip of her water and broke off a tiny piece of her biscuit. It was hard and bland, like one might expect of

a cookie that was called a "digestive." It tasted of vanilla—chalky, gritty vanilla.

But that was okay.

Because in seven hours—*wait, no, six and a half*, she realized, glancing at her watch—Abby's whole world was going to be a giant, gooey pint of New York Superfudge Chunk.

Well, except in London, of course.